MYSTERIES IN OUR NATIONAL PARKS

MYSTERY
#1

MYSTERIES
IN OUR NATIONAL PARKS

Wolf Stalker

GLORIA SKURZYNSKI AND ALANE FERGUSON

NATIONAL GEOGRAPHIC SOCIETY
WASHINGTON, D.C.

For Barbara Lalicki

Together again, the three of us

This is a work of fiction. Any resemblance to living persons or events other than
descriptions of natural phenomena is purely coincidental.

Map by Matthew Frey—Wood Ronsaville Harlin, Inc.
Book design by Ivy Pages.

Library of Congress Cataloging-in-Publication Data
Skurzynski, Gloria
    Wolf stalker / Gloria Skurzynski and Alane Ferguson
    p. cm. —(A national parks mystery ; #1)
    Summary: Twelve-year-old Jack, his younger sister, and the family's
teenage foster child Troy go to Yellowstone National Park, where Jack's mother, a wildlife veterinarian, is
investigating the report that wolves reintroduced to the park have killed a dog there.
        ISBN 0-7922-7034-7 (hardcover)
        ISBN 0-7922-7652-3 (paperback)
        [1. Wolves—Fiction.   2. Wildlife reintroduction—Fiction.
    3. Wildlife conservation—Fiction. 4. Yellowstone National Park—Fiction. 5. National parks and
reserves—Fiction. 6. Mystery and detective stories.]
    I. Ferguson, Alane. II. Title. III. Series.
    PZ7.S6287Wo   1997   97-11125
    [Fic]—DC21

Printed in the United States of America

Acknowledgments

The authors are grateful for the valuable

information provided so generously by

Mike Phillips, Wolf Restoration Program Leader,

Yellowstone National Park;

Marsha Karle, Chief of Public Affairs,

Yellowstone National Park;

Elden Naranjo, Tribal Historian for

the Southern Ute Tribe;

Bruce L. Smith, Wildlife Biologist,

National Elk Refuge, Jackson, Wyoming;

and Larry F. Jones, ballistics expert.

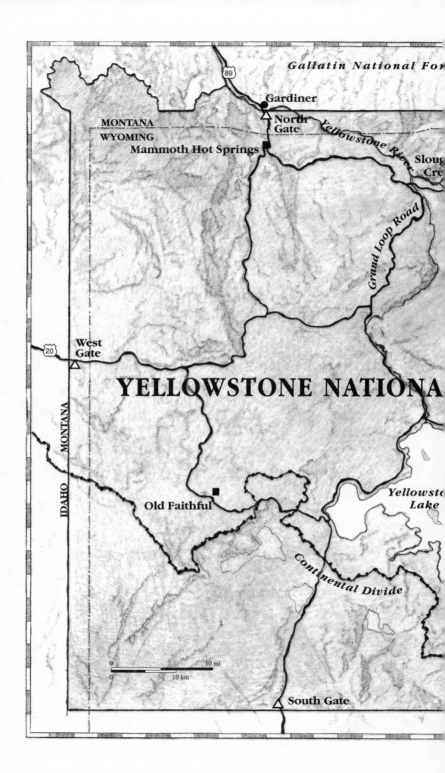

Park Data

States:
Wyoming, Idaho,
and Montana

Established:
1872

Area:
2,221,766 acres;
UNESCO world heritage
site and international
biosphere reserve

Climate:
Summers short and
cool, winters harsh

Natural Features:
Thousands of
geothermal features;
rugged mountains;
alpine lakes;
deep river canyons;
waterfalls

A soulful howl rose, fell, and then faded. It told the man he was zeroing in on his prey. As he fingered the barrel of his rifle, his eyes searched the thick forest growth for signs of his enemy. There! A flash of black fur followed by a streak of silver—instantly he raised his rifle, but before he could take aim, the wolves disappeared into the brush. Once again, they had escaped his bullet.

"Don't care how long it takes," he murmured. "You're mine." Slinging his rifle across his shoulder, the man impatiently pushed at branches hanging in his line of sight. Morning light dappled Yellowstone National Park, turning the autumn grass into pale gold. Intent on his quest, the man didn't notice.

He was the stalker; the wolves, his prey....

CHAPTER ONE

Can't you put some quarters in the slot or something to make it shoot off?" Troy asked. "We've been waiting forever."

Jack looked up sharply.

He didn't know Troy well enough to tell if he was joking. Ashley, though, burst out laughing.

"Mom!" she yelled. "Troy said we should put money in a slot to make Old Faithful start. Like it was a video game or something. Isn't that funny?"

Olivia Landon smiled, but Jack could tell his mother was distracted. She stared intently at a cellular phone she was holding. "Mmm," she murmured, which meant she hadn't really noticed what anyone was saying.

Ashley tried again. "Mom—"

Suddenly, their mother seemed to focus. "I'm sorry, honey. It's just—every minute that slips by makes it harder for me to analyze the killing scene." Turning the cell phone in her hand, she frowned and said, "I should have gotten the call an hour ago. I hope nothing's gone wrong...."

"So what are we supposed to do in the meantime—just stand here forever?" Troy growled.

Jack felt his stomach clamp with anger. He wished he could dump Troy right into Old Faithful and watch him melt, but his father's expression warned him to keep quiet.

Steven Landon explained, "Until Mike's call comes, we might as well stay here." Mike was the head of Yellowstone's Wolf Restoration Program. The Landons were supposed to meet him that afternoon, but they didn't know where. "Meanwhile, we can watch Old Faithful erupt," Steven added.

"Watch what? Nothing's happening," Troy said.

Olivia patted the bench, inviting Troy to sit beside her. But of course he wouldn't. He kept standing there. "Don't worry, Troy," she began. "It will happen—"

Fists jammed into the pockets of his cheap bomber jacket, Troy walked away.

Olivia and Steven Landon exchanged glances. Their look meant that Troy Haverson had better be watched. They were responsible for him. He was their temporary foster child.

"Will you go after him, Steven?" Olivia asked. "I want to dial Mike's number again. I can't figure out why I haven't heard from him."

"No problem. I'll get Troy." Steven ambled after the

scowling boy, and when he caught up to him, put his hand on Troy's shoulder. "Old Faithful will start up any minute now," he said. "It's pretty spectacular—you'll want to see the whole thing right from the beginning."

"Who says?" Troy muttered, but he let Steven lead him back toward the Landon family group.

Luckily, right then Old Faithful did begin to rumble. Gurgling, splashing, it slid tentative, watery fingers aboveground. Then, as if to test the world of daylight, the first narrow column of water and steam rushed up, and a cheer rose from the hundreds of visitors ringed around the viewing area.

After the watery column fell back, sudden bursts bubbled up one right after the other, making sounds like waves on a seashore. They rose, fell, and rose again to even greater heights. Puffs of vapor at the top of the column got caught by wind, while the heavier drops splashed back onto the ground. At the peak of the eruption, Old Faithful shot nearly 200 feet into the clear blue sky, looking as if it might touch a cloud, just as white, that floated overhead. Roaring, throbbing, the column of water and steam widened into a wall of mist that drifted like a curtain across a stage before it began its descent. Slowly subsiding, it fell to earth to collect underground for the next performance. In another hour—more or less.

"Ten thousand gallons of superheated steam— wow!" Steven exclaimed.

"The early Indians called this place 'water that keeps on coming out,'" Ashley said. "How'd you like it, Troy?"

If Troy was impressed, he wasn't going to admit it. Ignoring Ashley, he asked Steven, "So why didn't you take pictures? You're supposed to be a photographer."

"He's a great photographer," Jack declared.

"At home I've got lots of shots of Old Faithful. Mostly, now, I photograph wildlife. Elk and bison and mountain lions—"

"Yeah?" Troy shrugged. "They told me you just work in some fast-photo shop developing film."

Steven flushed a little, but he answered patiently, "That's my day job. If I could make a living photographing animals full-time, that's what I'd do."

Jack couldn't stand it. Why was his father being so polite? And so was his mother, and so was his sister Ashley, as if Troy were some special, important guest the Landon family had to fuss over and make as welcome as possible, instead of just the obnoxious punk kid that he really was.

Almost from the first minute he'd met him, Jack had wanted to take a punch at Troy.

When the doorbell rang the night before, all the Landons had gathered in the entryway. After taking a deep breath, Olivia reached out to open the front door wide.

"Hi. I'm Theresa Lopez," a woman with curling gray hair had said, at the same time grabbing the area right above Troy's elbow to lead him inside. "And this is Troy Haverson."

Shuffling, head down, Troy hung back behind the social worker. Right off, Jack could tell he didn't have a lot of money. Not that the Landon family did either, but Troy looked different, more raw than the kids who lived in Jack's neighborhood. His black bomber jacket was plastic, not leather; the kind with cheap silver zippers that didn't close right. His sneakers were so worn the sides had pulled away from the canvas like strips of rubber lettuce. On the step next to him was a cardboard box he was using as a suitcase. Bands of duct tape had been wrapped around it; on top, the tape looped into a makeshift handle.

Jack wanted to smile at Troy, to try to be nice so his dad would be pleased. It was Steven's idea that the family take in short-term foster kids, to "put something back into the system," as Steven phrased it. But Troy kept his eyes down and his face turned away.

Looking grave, the social worker said, "This guy has had a pretty rough go of it, but I know he's going to be fine. He really appreciates you helping him out on such short notice. Right, Troy?"

"Mm." Troy pulled his hands from his pockets, crunching his fists tightly against his sides. Squeeze, relax, squeeze, relax; it was as if he could barely hold himself together inside his skin.

He was tall, taller than Jack, and thicker in the chest

and arms. Even though he was only 13, a faint mustache shadowed his upper lip. Dark eyebrows knit over the bridge of his nose. For an instant his chin bobbed up; wary brown eyes skimmed the Landon family, then dropped again. Stringy hair hung over Troy's face like a curtain drawn against intruders. To Jack, the boy looked meaner than a trash dog. How long, Jack wondered, was this shelter kid going to need sheltering?

"Great to meet you, Troy," Steven Landon said heartily. "You're welcome here."

"Yes, Troy, we're all so happy to meet you," Olivia told him.

Ignoring her, Troy asked flatly, "When can I go to my room?" A looked passed between Jack's mother and father and the social worker until it came around and rested on Troy once again.

"How about now?" Steven answered. "Son, take Troy to where he's staying, and make sure you show him the bathroom and the kitchen while you're at it. Your mother and I need to talk to Ms. Lopez for a minute."

Troy grabbed the duct-tape handle and followed Jack down the hallway. Brushing past Jack, he walked into the guest room just as Jack was about to announce, "This is it."

In the silence, Troy's glance darted around the room. Jack tried again. "The bathroom's through that door, and the kitchen's—"

"The room with the refrigerator, right?" Shaking his head, Troy snorted as if Jack were the stupidest person in the world. He didn't seem to notice the navy bed-spread Olivia Landon had so carefully washed and smoothed out, or the wicker basket filled with apples Steven had placed on the dresser, or the computer banner Ashley'd made to welcome him.

"Okay," Jack said slowly. "So you've already figured out our house. Do you need anything else?" He hoped the answer would be no, because all he wanted was to escape into his own room and hide.

Troy flopped onto the bed. He kicked off one shoe by using the toe of his other foot. The worn sneaker flew into the air before hitting the wall with a thud.

Repeating the process on the other shoe, he asked, "So what did they say about me? Did they tell you my mom just walked out the door and didn't come back?"

Taken by surprise, Jack didn't know what to answer. He just nodded.

"Liars. They're all a bunch of freakin' liars. My mom would never leave me. Never."

But she had. According to the report given to the Landon family by the Department of Social Services, Troy's mother had simply disappeared, leaving him all alone, with no food and no money.

"Something bad must have happened to her," Troy insisted.

"Did you tell the police?" Jack asked.

Troy laughed, but it wasn't a happy sound. "Yeah—I stayed on my own for two days, then I called the cops. Big mistake. They took down all the stuff I told them, and then they asked who was stayin' with me and I said 'No one. I can handle it. You guys just find my mom.' So instead the cops called the Social Services and they came and got me."

"Well, when your mom comes back, they'll let her know where you are and everything'll work out OK."

"Don't you listen?" Anger crackled from his voice and his dark eyes. Jack had never met anyone who seethed the way Troy seemed to, as if emotional lava was roiling just beneath his skin and any second could erupt. "My—mom's—in—some—kind—of—trouble! I need to be home so I can find her."

"But you can't stay all by yourself."

"Why not? I don't need anybody." Leaning back, Troy knit his fingers together and rested his head in them. Suddenly Ashley came bowling into the room and ran smack into Jack's back.

"Sorry, Jack. Hi, Troy."

Troy gave Ashley a little wave, but to Jack it looked more like a put-down than a hello.

"Jack, guess what?" Ashley exclaimed. "Something happened! Didn't you hear the phone?"

"No."

"Mom got a call, and this guy says wolves came

down and ate his dog even though it wasn't doing anything and it's been on talk radio and stuff and now they need Mom to figure out what happened."

"Does she always talk so fast?" Troy asked.

She did, but Jack didn't like Troy enough to tell him so.

"Ms. Lopez told Mom it's OK to take Troy with us, but we have to get ready right away. We need to hurry up and pack!"

"Wait a minute, did she just say I'm going somewhere?" Troy demanded. "No way!"

Ashley's large brown eyes widened even more. "But we've got to go! If we don't, they might kill all the wolves!"

"Hold it!" Jack said, taking her arm. "Just slow down and start again. Where are we going?"

"To save the wolves. We're leaving tomorrow morning, first thing."

"What wolves?"

"Didn't you listen?" Exasperated, looking from Jack to Troy and back, Ashley said, "The wolves they put in the park. They're saying they're too wild and mean. They're saying that the wolves are gonna start killing people next. Mom said that's not right, so that's why we're going there."

"Going where?" Jack yelled.

"I already told you where. The park! Yellowstone."

At that minute Olivia and Steven came crowding into the room behind Ashley. Jack knew how to read his mother's eyes, and he could see that Olivia had become energized by this crisis, whatever it was. "Can you believe it?" she asked. "It's lucky they called me on a weekend because now we can all go together. Tomorrow's Saturday—we ought to be back late Sunday so you kids won't miss any school."

"We need to be packed and in the car no later than seven tomorrow morning—" Steven began, but Troy broke in.

"I'm outta here right now," he said, jumping up from the bed. "No way am I gonna leave this town until I find my mom." He would have rushed out of the room if Steven hadn't shut the door hard and leaned against it from the inside.

"Outta my way, man!" Troy ordered.

Steven Landon knew how to approach frightened animals without threatening them. As if Troy were a cornered deer, he locked eyes with the boy, then slowly raised his hand, palm up. In a quiet voice Steven told him, "I think I know how you must feel, Troy. But if you leave here right now, the police will pick you up and you'll spend the weekend in juvenile hall. And what good would that do anyone?"

Steven took a step closer. "Come with us, Troy. We'll stay in phone contact with your social worker. As soon as there's any news about your mother, you'll be the first to find out. I promise."

Troy no longer looked like a frightened animal, he

looked like a caged animal. Coiled in a half-crouch, color staining his cheeks, he shouted, "This is supposed to be my room, right? Why are all of you in here? If I gotta be stuck with you in a car tomorrow, you need to give me some space now." His voice broke. "OK?"

"Right!" Gesturing for her family to leave, Olivia said, "Let's get started packing, kids. Tomorrow will begin early."

Too early. By six that Saturday morning, at the day's first pale light, Jack was fighting to hang onto his pillow while his father dragged him out of bed.

By seven, as the rosy glow from the sunrise lingered over the jagged, snow-capped peaks of the Grand Teton Mountain Range, all the Landons plus Troy were crowded into their jeep, heading for Yellowstone.

CHAPTER TWO

"**D**id you get hold of Mike?" Jack asked his mother.

Olivia shook her head. Her mouth pressed into a thin line. "I am definitely getting worried. Something must have gone wrong. I think we better drive up to the wolf office."

It was the weekend after Labor Day. Although Yellowstone still had plenty of visitors, the crowds were skimpy compared with the holiday jam-up a week earlier. Jack had been on this same walkway between Old Faithful and the parking lot when actual human gridlock occurred, and no one could move at all. Those times, he'd kept his eyes focused on his father's blond head. At six foot three, Steven was pretty easy to follow in a crowd. Olivia got swallowed.

Jack looked like his father: tall, thin, and blond. Ashley was a young version of her mother: short and slightly built, with big dark eyes and dark hair that framed her face in gentle wisps. And right now, Ashley was babbling to strangers, the way she always did. In the stream of visitors heading for their cars, Ashley had picked out a silver-haired couple. Tagging along beside them, she said, "Wasn't it great?"

"Fantastic," the woman agreed.

"Have you ever seen it before?"

"No. We live in Minnesota," the man answered.

Smiling, the woman asked, "So did you come to Yellowstone just to watch Old Faithful?"

"No, we're here to help the wolves. My mom's a wildlife veterinarian."

"Really?"

"Uh-huh. She works at the National Elk Refuge in Jackson Hole, but sometimes she gets a call and she has to help the national parks in emergencies..."

That Ashley! Jack thought. As a baby, she'd always smiled at everyone she saw. Now here she was, almost 11, and still acting as though each person who crossed her path was a new friend just waiting to be discovered.

Jack wasn't as trusting. Whenever they were out together, he made it his job to keep an eye on his sister, trying to prevent her from spilling the entire life stories of all the Landons into the ears of total strangers. This couple looked harmless enough—the man wore the usual tourist camera slung around his neck, and a floppy-brimmed hat on his head; his wife had on a pink sweatshirt that said Save the Whales. It matched the sun-tinted pink of her cheeks.

"Well, my husband and I love wolves. They have every right to be here in Yellowstone," the woman told her.

"That's what my mom thinks. It's not their fault if a dog tries to mess with them."

"Ashley—" Olivia began.

"It's true! Isn't that why we came here, Mom? Because that dog got killed yesterday by the wolves?" Turning back to the couple, Ashley said, "My mom's investigating to find out what really happened when the dog got eaten, but it might be hard to tell if there's not much left of him."

"Goodness!" the woman said. "So you're the one who's investigating?" she asked Olivia.

Giving Ashley a look, Olivia hesitated before she answered, "I'm mostly here to gather some information. I hope to handle it quietly, so people won't hear about the killing and become upset at the wolves."

The man said, "Well, if you wanted to keep it a secret, you're too late. I already heard about that wolf attack on the national news."

Olivia squeezed her eyes shut. "Oh, no."

"And I ought to warn you—you're going to be right in the middle of a big mess. When we came into the park this morning, demonstrators were picketing. Right outside the west gate. The news people were all over the place with TV cameras and everything."

The man and woman took turns interrupting each other as they told the story: "People were carrying signs and yelling—"

"'Get rid of the wolves, or we'll do it for you—'"

"—and, 'The only good wolf is a dead wolf.'"

"Who were these people?" Steven asked.

"Looked like a bunch of ranchers to me. From what their signs said, wolves have been eating their sheep and they don't like it."

"No, no, no," the woman interrupted. "Ranchers were there, too, but most of the people were some kind of militia group. There are a lot of baldhead militia groups in this part of the country—"

The man laughed. "They're called skinheads, Louise. Not baldheads."

"Whatever. They kept yelling that bringing wolves to the park was government interference, and citizens' rights were being trampled on—"

By then they'd all reached the Landons' jeep in the parking lot. Troy lounged against the tailgate, looking bored, while Olivia and Steven extracted every bit of information they could from the Minnesota couple. As they parted, the woman called back, "We believe the wolves should be in Yellowstone, particularly since they were here first. But I think you're going to have a real battle keeping them in the park."

"They're worth fighting for," Olivia answered. She unlocked the door and said, "Get in the jeep, kids. We need to find out what's been going on around here."

On the way to Yellowstone, Jack had been stuck for four long hours sitting in the back seat beside sullen, surly Troy Haverson. Ashley had it even worse: To leave enough room for the two boys, she'd been crammed into the jeep's tailgate, with backpacks and totes and extra parkas and Steven's cases of camera equipment. Now they were back in the jeep again, but this time they wouldn't have far to go.

Stands of lodgepole pine lined both sides of the road. Some clumps were tall and green. Others had been burned black from forest fires; their skinny trunks stood straight up like charred toothpicks. For anyone who hadn't seen it before, the evidence of fire's devastation must have been startling. But Troy stayed slumped in his corner, hardly noticing, saying nothing.

Steven was driving, which left Olivia free to turn around in her seat to tempt Troy into conversation—or at least into some kind of response. "This is probably all new to you, but the fight over the wolves goes way back. Did you know, Troy," she began, "that wolves roamed Yellowstone for thousands of years? Then when people first moved into this area more than a century ago, they killed the wolves for their pelts—you know, their fur?"

"Yeah, that's right, Mom." Ashley chimed in because she knew the story almost as well as her mother did. "After that, ranchers started poisoning the wolves because they chased after sheep and cattle. And pretty soon there weren't any wolves left. For more than 60 years, not a single wolf in all of Yellowstone. Now we've got them back again, but...." Her face clouded. "It sounds like they're in trouble."

Troy just looked out the window. Jack thought he wasn't going to answer at all, but then he muttered, "So wolves got screwed up when people started messing in their lives, right?"

Olivia hesitated. "Well...yes. I guess you could say that."

"And they would have been a whole lot better off if people had just left them alone. Right?"

It was a question that wasn't quite a question. Was he talking about the wolves or about himself, Jack wondered.

Olivia took the hint and left Troy to his own thoughts. She faced forward again, took out her cell phone, and punched in Mike's number. Once more she only got his answering machine. This time she didn't bother to leave a message.

Steven turned on the car radio, maybe so the two of them could talk about Troy without being overheard. Or talk about the wolves, or the demonstrators, or about what they were going to do now since they couldn't connect with Mike.

"Can't you put on some better music, Mom?" Jack asked. "That station's dumb."

"Yeah. Dumb," Ashley echoed.

"OK." Olivia started to change the dial on the car radio, but stopped abruptly.

"Listen!" she exclaimed.

"...question of wolves in Yellowstone. This is JJK-Talk Radio. Because of intense public interest, we're rebroadcasting last night's interview with Mr. George Campbell," an announcer was saying. "Campbell is the man whose dog was viciously attacked and killed by wolves in Yellowstone yesterday. All right, folks, here we go. And after we play this, we'll be ready to take your calls on this explosive issue." There was a slight clicking sound, and then, "You told us, Mr. Campbell, that you weren't actually in Yellowstone Park when your dog was murdered."

"That's right. I was hiking in Gallatin National Forest, which is right next to Yellowstone, when the wolves came after me and my dog."

"So," the announcer continued, "the wolf pack chased your golden retriever over the boundary line into Yellowstone."

"You got it, Gary. I paid five hundred dollars for that dog when he was a pup. After I trained him to hunt, he was worth a whole lot more than that. Rex was the best hunting dog I ever owned. That wolf pack ran him down and ripped him up, and there was nothin' I could do to save him. People better start being careful— before you know it, wolves'll be snatching your dogs off your front porch and babies outta their—"

"That's ridiculous!" Olivia was getting more upset. "Wolves don't—"

"Take it easy." Steven reached out his hand to calm her, then turned the radio louder.

"Mr. Campbell, there's been some question about Rex being found inside Yellowstone Park. Just so our listeners understand, dogs are allowed in Gallatin National Forest, where you said you were, but no dog is allowed to roam Yellowstone's back country. Not even on a leash."

"Yeah, but see, Gary, I wasn't in the park until after the wolves chased Rex across the boundary. I mean, I was close to Yellowstone, you know? Maybe even real close. But it was the wolves' fault Rex ran into the park. They chased him, and then they killed him."

Another click, and then the announcer said, "Okay, folks, that was last night. Now it's Saturday afternoon, we're on the air live, and all our lines are open. Just pick up your phones and punch in JJK-TALK. Remember, the JJ stands for Judge and Jury, and that means all of you great folks out there in our listening audience."

There was the sound of a ringing phone, followed by, "Here's our first caller: Martha from Billings. This is JJK-Talk Radio, Martha. Go ahead."

"Well...." A woman's voice crackled over the radio. "Uh—am I on the air, Gary?"

"You sure are, Martha. Go ahead."

"Well, I just want to say, those vicious wolves are the Adolf Hitler of the animal kingdom. I'm scared to let my kids stand on the corner to wait for the school bus anymore. Like Mr. Campbell said, what if a wolf or a whole pack of those killer wolves came running out of Yellowstone? No one is safe."

"All right, thanks for calling in, Martha. Let's get another opinion. This next caller is Larry from Pocatello. Larry's with a group that is picketing at Yellowstone right now to protest the wolves. That's pro-*test,* folks, not pro-tect! Go ahead, Larry. Tell us what you think."

In a deep, deliberate voice, the new caller declared, "When this country was founded, it was the people who decided what was done and what wasn't. Now everything's run by the government. A bunch of Washington suits sat down with some tree huggers and dictated that killer wolves should come back into our national park."

"So what's your point, Larry? Can you sum it up?" the announcer asked.

"The point is—the government's cramming this wolf thing down the regular citizen's throat. People, we don't have to take it! We got to unite and rid Yellowstone Park of those bloodthirsty wolves before it's too late!"

More phones rang in the background as the announcer asked, "Just how do you suggest we do that, Larry?"

"If I could, I'd say, 'Men, take up your rifles and go into Yellowstone and—'"

"I can't stand it!" Olivia cried, snapping off the radio. "How can people talk so crazy and get so worked up over this kind of hysterical propaganda?"

In the backseat, Troy glanced from Olivia to Steven and back again. For once, he seemed interested in what was going on.

"Just wait till we get to the site of the so-called wolf attack, Steven," Olivia vowed. "I'm going to reconstruct what happened with that dog. I have a feeling there's more to it than George Campbell is telling."

"You'll find out the truth, Mom," Ashley said confidently.

Steven shrugged. "The guy's dog is dead, Olivia. That much of it is true. Even the park officials admit the wolves killed the dog."

"Well, I still want to hear what Mike has to say," Olivia answered. "If I can ever get through to him."

Since Ashley was kneeling in the tailgate, she had a good view of the highway. "Watch out, Dad," she yelled. "Cars are stopping up ahead."

As they slowed down and drove closer, they could see the cause of the traffic pileup: three big, shaggy, bearded bison were standing in the middle of the road. Cars from both directions had stopped in long lines; doors were flung open as people jumped out, cameras in hand, to take pictures of the massive beasts.

"Don't the visitors read the warnings?" Olivia asked, exasperated. She rolled down the window on her side of the jeep and leaned out—head, shoulders, and torso. "Stay away from those bison!" she yelled to the people on the road. "They can charge you and gore you. Please! You're putting yourselves in danger."

A few people turned to stare at Olivia, but most of them just kept taking pictures.

"Listen to me! Those bison look big and slow, but they can move fast. Thirty miles an hour!"

"Give it up, Mom," Jack said, embarrassed that his mother was sticking out of the jeep window like a jack-in-the-box, waving her arms and shouting that way, especially since no one seemed to be taking her seriously. Only the big bull buffalo raised his head to stare at Olivia with his beady eyes. Slowly, he shook his massive head, as if agreeing with Olivia that tourists could be unbelievably, dangerously reckless. Rippling the dust off his dark hide, he turned and trotted down an embankment into the field below. His pair of buffalo cows followed him.

Taking their time, people returned to their cars. Doors slammed and motors revved up as the caravans started out once more, now that the unexpected bison appearance had ended. When the Landon jeep finally got moving again, they'd lost close to 15 minutes. Olivia began to chew her fingertip.

"What time were you supposed to meet Mike?" Jack asked.

"Around noon. But I can't get him to answer his

phone, and it's already almost two o'clock. I've left my cell phone number on his machine four times already! The problem is he never told me where we were supposed to meet him—he just said to phone him when we got close. This is so frustrating!"

"Look, he knows we're coming, and you've done everything you can. I think the best plan is to go to the wolf office like you suggested," Steven said.

"Where's that?" Ashley wanted to know.

"Close to Mammoth Hot Springs. Just down a side road."

"I love that place!" Ashley exclaimed. "Can I show Mammoth Hot Springs to Troy? Wait till you see it, Troy. It's like a great big layer cake with lots of different colored icing."

Why bother, Jack thought. Even though Troy had never before been to Yellowstone because he'd lived in Wyoming for only a couple of months, he seemed totally bored by everything they'd seen so far. When he condescended to look at anything, it was with expressionless eyes, through half-lowered lids.

"Sorry, Ashley," Steven began, "I don't think we can fit that in right now. Your mother has to handle the wolf crisis—"

"Oh, go ahead and take them," Olivia interrupted. "I'm a little tense over this whole thing, Steven. It really might be better to just drop me off at the wolf office while the rest of you take a quick look at Mammoth

Hot Springs. I'll try to get all the details before you come back for me—like, where's Mike, and what's happening with those demonstrators!"

Within the next half hour, Steven took Olivia to the wolf restoration office, parked the car near Mammoth Hot Springs, and shepherded his own two kids and a reluctant Troy along the boardwalk.

Water didn't shoot up into the air in Mammoth Hot Springs. It flowed up or brimmed over from cracks in the surface. On the flat topmost terrace, which seemed wide enough to make a table for all the gods and giants of Olympus, steam rose in gentle wisps. Since each day two tons of water-dissolved minerals bubbled up and got deposited on the crust, Mammoth Hot Springs looked different in shape and color every time Jack saw it.

Ashley stood next to Troy at the railing and said, "See how the water comes up? It's full of—what do you call it, Dad? I never remember."

Before Steven could answer, Jack did. He had decided he should teach Troy a fact or two about the natural wonders of Yellowstone, especially since Troy was from the city and wouldn't know anything about hot springs. Loudly enough that the tourists around him could hear, too, he announced, "It's calcium carbonate, Ashley. That's what the water's full of—calcium carbonate."

"From limestone," Troy said.

Jack looked at him in disbelief. Who'd have thought

Troy would know that? "Not really," Jack said stiffly, still talking loud. "The carbonate dissolves out from the calcium when it gets on the surface. What's left—that's the stuff that builds up these terraces—is called travertine."

"Yeah, but it starts out from limestone and limestone's white," Troy said, "so how come some of the rocks look pink and green and orange?"

"What a great question, Troy," Steven exclaimed, making Jack want to grind his teeth. "The colors come from different kinds of bacteria and algae that have adapted to survive in really hot water. I have some books about it at home—when we get back, we can look it up. But now we better drive back and get Olivia before we get into hot water. She's probably waiting for us."

At the wolf office building, Olivia was sitting on the front steps, her crossed arms leaning against her knees. When she saw them she cried, "Don't get out. Don't even stop the car—we have to leave right away and meet Mike."

As she reached to open the jeep's front door, Troy leaped out of the back.

"I'm not going," he said.

Jack groaned. Why did Troy have to be so difficult?

"What's wrong, Troy?" Ashley asked.

"What about my mom? I want to find out if the police have heard anything.

Steven cleared his throat. "That's reasonable, Troy.

I'll run inside and use their phone, but maybe I'll call Social Services instead of the police. They'll know what's happening."

"Why can't you use Olivia's phone?"

"Because it won't reach that far. I've tried to call Jackson Hole on the wireless cell phone, but all these mountains around here cause interference. The signal gets blocked. So I need to use a regular phone, with wires. Okay?"

Troy nodded, and watched as Steven climbed the few steps into the relocation office. Olivia started to explain to the kids that Mike had already gone ahead, and they were to meet him at Slough Creek.

"I'm tired of riding in the tailgate, Mom," Ashley complained. "How far is it to Stew Creek?"

"Not Stew Creek," Olivia corrected her. "Slough Creek. It's spelled S-L-O-U-G-H, but it's pronounced like 'he slew the dragon.' And we'll be there in less than half an hour."

His eyes trained on the building in front of him, Troy twisted an end of his T-shirt into a thin rope. When he let it go, it fell into a mass of wrinkles. Finally, the screen door swung open and Steven clattered down the steps, shaking his head. "No news," he said. "I'm sorry, Troy."

Quietly, they took their places back inside the jeep. During the half-hour drive to Slough Creek, they kept their voices low—that is, the Landons did. Troy didn't talk at all. "I did get some more information about the dog's death," Olivia told them. "They know wolves were in the area where the dog was supposed to have been killed. But they lost contact with one of the wolves, a young male. His radio collar stopped transmitting. He could have wiggled out of it, or the batteries might have failed, or—"

"Maybe he got killed, too," Jack said.

"Mmmm, that wouldn't be why the collar stopped transmitting. When a wolf doesn't move for four hours, the radio collar goes into what's called 'mortality mode'—it gives off a really rapid signal. This wolf's collar just stopped working, period. The whole thing's kind of mysterious."

The Landons discussed the possibilities, but Troy didn't speak or move. He just sat with his hand over his eyes. Jack wondered if maybe he was crying about his mother. But no, a tough kid like Troy would never cry.

CHAPTER THREE

After they turned off the highway, they drove a few more miles down a dirt road to a parking lot in the middle of nowhere. A very odd place for a parking lot, Jack thought. But several campers and vans stood there, so people must have left their vehicles behind while they hiked the trails.

"This time everybody can get out and stay out," Olivia said. "Because there's Mike, waiting for us."

A man came toward them.

The first thing Jack noticed was the man's cap, decorated with a logo of a wolf and the words Project Wolfstock, Yellowstone—definitely not part of the regulation Park Service uniform, but cool.

The second thing Jack noticed was Mike's expression. He looked very surprised to see all of them. "What's with the kids?" he asked.

It was Olivia's turn to look surprised. "Didn't you

get my messages? I called and left several voice messages on your answering machine—that we were bringing our own two kids and an extra one."

"Shoot, Olivia," Mike exclaimed. He took off his cap and scratched his head. "You wouldn't believe the kind of day this has been! I've been out of the office all day because of all the trouble—demonstrators picketing, and about a zillion news reporters—"

"We heard about it," Steven told him.

"I never even had a chance to check my voice messages," Mike apologized. "Anyway, I figured it was just the two you of you coming, so I only brought three horses. I wish we could take the kids with us—kids have such sharp eyes, they might notice things we miss—but there's no time now to go back for more horses. If we don't get started, we're gonna run out of daylight."

The tall horses were already saddled and waiting, stamping, snorting, and touching each other neck-to-neck. Their reins were looped around hooks on a red trailer that was hitched to a Park Service truck.

"That's OK," Steven said. "I'll just stay here with the kids while you and Olivia ride up to the site."

"No, Steve, that won't work. I need you to take pictures of the scene. And we need to get there as fast as possible." Mike tugged the brim of his cap, pulling it down to his eyebrows. "Not just because of the light, but because of scavengers getting at that dead dog's remains. Every minute we wait, another raven comes to feed on the carcass. If we don't get there soon to examine the area and take some good pictures, the evidence will be gone."

Jack interrupted, "It's OK, Mom and Dad. Us kids'll just hang out here till you get back." Before he even finished, he saw Steven shake his head.

"Can't do that," Steven said.

"Why not?" Mike asked. "They're big kids."

"No. Definitely no," Olivia declared.

Troy scowled. "Because of me, right? You think I'm gonna run. Where would I go, around here?" He gestured at the steep hills that rose into even steeper mountains, covered with pines and thick scrub.

No one answered, because all of them knew that the road they'd driven in on cut through those mountains, right back to the highway only a couple of miles away. Troy could easily hike back and thumb a ride. With the grown-ups gone, there was no way Jack and Ashley would be able stop him.

"Tell you what," Mike said. "Since you brought your cell phone, I'll call over to headquarters and have one of the park rangers come by to get the kids. Nicole," he said to Olivia. "That's her name. In fact, right now she's not far from here, at Roosevelt Lodge. She can drive here in ten minutes." When Olivia unfolded the small phone and handed it to him, Mike dialed the number.

They couldn't hear what he was saying into the

phone because Steven gathered the three kids around him and started talking. "I don't know how this is going to work out for you guys," he said. "I'm not sure how long we'll be gone."

"Probably four or five hours," Olivia broke in.

"Ask Nicole to take you straight to Roosevelt Lodge," Steven decided. "She'll stay with you until we get back. I'll give you money so you can get something to eat." Jack and Ashley nodded.

Mike snapped the phone shut and gave it back to Olivia. "It's all set," he told them. "Nicole's on her way. You kids wait right here beside the truck."

"How will we know it's Nicole and not a stranger?" Ashley asked.

Mike grinned at her. "Because she'll be wearing a national park ranger's uniform with a name tag that says 'Nicole Hardy.' That's how you'll know. OK?"

Ashley smiled back at him. "Just checking."

While Steven loaded his camera equipment into the saddlepacks of one of the horses, Olivia adjusted the stirrups on another one.

"I forgot you're a short person," Mike teased her, "or I would have pulled those stirrups way up high." He looked at his watch. "We need to mount up and get moving. Nicole should be here in about two minutes. The kids'll be all right for that long."

From high in her saddle, Olivia looked down at Jack and Ashley. Jack could tell his mother was worried.

"Mom, we'll be fine," he echoed. "We'll stay right here till the ranger comes. Promise."

With a creak of saddle leather and the crunch of hoofs on gravel, the three horses moved out of the parking lot, toward the banks of Slough Creek. Steven was already deep in conversation with Mike. Olivia turned to wave and called out, "Take care, OK?"

After the adults were out of sight, Troy kicked at some rocks. Then he picked up half a dozen stones and threw them, one at a time, hitting a metal sign that showed a circle with a crossbar across a picture of a dog on a leash. "No dogs," it meant. Not even on leashes.

Bored with that, Troy climbed onto a fender of the horse trailer and peered inside. Next he tested the door of the Park Service truck, but it was locked. "How long are we supposed to wait here?" he grumbled.

Ashley was rummaging through the tailgate of the jeep, searching for something to eat. "Look, Jack," she called out. "Here's my parka and your parka and here's Dad's old red one. I bet Mom packed that for Troy, 'cause it'll get cold tonight." She held it up for Troy to see.

Troy sniffed disdainfully. "You think I'd wear that? No way! It's red!"

"Just wait," Jack said, "till the temperature drops really low and we're in a cabin tonight and you have to go to the bathroom—which is about a block away from the cabins. You'll wear it."

"I wear black," Troy said.

It wasn't worth arguing about. Jack didn't have a watch on, but it seemed to him that Nicole, the ranger, should have reached them by now. Tree shadows were beginning to lengthen; the sun hung halfway down the sky.

"Bring my backpack when you get out of the jeep," he told Ashley. He had a new issue of *Photography Today* in it; while he was waiting, he might as well give it a look-through.

Dragging her parka and Jack's along with Jack's pack, Ashley backed out of the jeep. When her feet touched the ground, she slammed the door. Immediately she said, "Oh-oh," and looked worried.

"What?" Jack asked.

"I think I kicked the lock button on my way out." She tested the jeep doors. "Yep. It's all locked up. Can't get in."

"Doesn't matter," Jack said. "We don't need anything from in there. The ranger's going to take us to Roosevelt Lodge and Dad already gave me money for dinner. It's in my pocket."

"Where is she?" Ashley wondered.

"She'll get here soon," Jack answered, and opened his magazine.

More minutes dragged by. "I want to see some wolves," Troy announced. "Your mom said there were wolves in this part of Yellowstone."

"We have to stay here," Jack said, not looking up.

"I'm just gonna walk along the creek and look for wolves." Troy narrowed his eyes as if challenging Jack to try to stop him.

The creek was only a couple of hundred yards away, close enough that the ranger could easily see them when she arrived.

Even though his father hadn't instructed him to, Jack knew he'd better stick pretty close to Troy. "I'm going with him. Ashley, you wait here for the ranger."

"Forget that! I'm not staying all by myself in this parking lot with the jeep locked so I can't get inside," Ashley answered. "If you're going, I'm going too."

Jack hesitated, but only for a minute, because Troy was running toward the creek bank. If he climbed down the bank, Jack might lose sight of him. "OK," he told Ashley, "you can come. But bring—" He stopped to think what he ought to take with them. Always prepare for the worst—that was his mother's motto. If they started fooling around near the creek bed, Ashley might fall in, and the water was cold. "Bring your parka," he ordered her. "Mine too. And my backpack. It's right there."

Ashley wrinkled her nose at him. "If you want it, you can carry it. I'm not carrying your backpack for you."

Jack said, "No one asked you to, tick-brain. And I want it because my camera's in it, and hurry up because I need to catch up to Troy so he won't get lost."

"Lost?" Ashley began to protest. "How can he—?"

"Just COME!" Jack grabbed his backpack and took off, not even waiting to see whether Ashley followed. After a minute he heard her footsteps behind him, but Troy was getting harder to see because he'd gone behind some trees. Between the branches, Jack caught flashes of Troy's shiny black jacket. It was moving away from them, fast.

That jerk Troy! He was heading down the nature trail!

He was close now. As the wolf and his mate sniffed the air, the man squinted through his rifle scope, locking on the silver wolf's forehead. "Hold on...hold on," he whispered as his finger found the trigger. Suddenly the wolf bolted out of his crosshairs and cantered down the mountain. "Demon wolves," the man muttered. "Don't matter. You'll be dead soon enough."

Below him, the man could see Slough Creek glittering in the afternoon sun. He knew its nearness made his plan risky, and for a moment he considered turning back. Then, his jaw tightening with resolve, he concentrated on his objective: the execution of the wolf.

Cussing under his breath, Jack ran along the dirt path. Or tried to run. Every hundred feet, it seemed, the trail was blocked by a fallen tree. Some of them were low enough to the ground that he could jump over them; others he had to stop and climb over. Twice his backpack caught on branches; once it got jerked right off his arm and landed hard on the path. When Jack worriedly opened the pack to make sure his camera hadn't been damaged, Ashley caught up to him.

"Isn't it pretty here?" she asked. She pointed to the ground cover, just beginning to take on its autumn colors; to small lavender asters growing against the roots of a toppled pine; at the wide, shallow creek that rippled serenely on their left, reflecting sky and clouds and the thick stands of evergreens that grew along its banks.

"Who cares about pretty!" Jack exploded. "When I catch up to that—That—He's nothing but trouble!"

"Troy just wants to see some wolves," Ashley said quietly.

"And what are the chances?" Jack cried. "Even if you catch a look at wolves, they're always so far away you can't see much, and Troy's such a dumb city kid he probably wouldn't know the difference between a coyote and a wolf even if he fell over one."

Jack wrapped a pair of socks around his camera and stuffed it back inside his backpack. His camping pack was always stocked with things like extra socks that his mother made him carry.

With Ashley behind him, he started out at a fast clip because he'd already lost too many minutes. Troy'd had plenty of time to get away. He could have bolted into the trees, or up the side of mountain, or across the creek without leaving any tracks that Jack could follow.

But only a hundred yards ahead, as Jack hurried

around a bend in the trail, he nearly bumped into Troy. Standing perfectly still, deep in the shadow of the trees, Troy was watching a young mule deer graze beside the creek.

"Back off and shut up," he muttered.

Ordinarily Jack would have shouted insults at him, would have vented his rage at Troy for causing so much trouble and for being, in general, a total creep. But Jack had been trained from babyhood to tread softly around animals in the wild, to never startle them or disturb their feeding. He clenched his teeth and his fists and managed to stay silent.

The yearling deer grazed peacefully in the mottled sunlight, switching his long ears forward and backward like a jackrabbit, and flicking his skinny white tail.

A perfect picture, Jack thought, if he could only get to his camera. As carefully as he could, he lifted the flap of his backpack, but in the stillness, the Velcro fastener pulling apart sounded like a string of exploding firecrackers.

The deer's head shot up.

For a moment it stared first at Ashley, next at Troy. Then, while Jack fumbled inside his pack for the camera, the young deer bounded away, splashing across the creek to the other bank, where four more mule deer, all adults, stood grazing.

"Crud!" Jack exclaimed in disgust. "What a great shot—and I missed it."

"They're right over there in the meadow," Ashley told him. "You can still take a picture."

"From this far away it wouldn't show anything. I'm really mad 'cause it was right in front of me and I blew it," Jack complained. He'd brought only his little point-and-shoot automatic camera that was no good for distance shots. "Anyway, we need to get back. Come on, Troy."

Troy ignored him. Big surprise.

"That ranger's probably already there by now, and when she doesn't find us she'll call Mom and Dad and Mike on the cell phone and they'll get all worried—"

"She can't," Ashley declared.

"Can't what?"

"Get ahold of Mom and Dad and Mike. Our cell phone's locked inside the jeep, remember? Mom didn't take it."

Whirling on them, Troy hissed, "Shut up! Something's happening over there."

Loudly, Ashley asked, "Over where? What?"

"I said shut up!" He gestured across the creek to the meadow, where the grass was no longer green, but had turned yellow with the near arrival of autumn.

"What? Deer?" Ashley asked.

Troy shook his head. He dropped to his knees and crouched behind the fallen log. Following the direction of Troy's intense stare, Jack saw—wolves! Two of them. One black and one gray.

The four large mule deer and the younger, smaller

one had seen the wolves, too. They started to move away, at first ambling slowly, then running faster as the two wolves loped diagonally across the meadow toward them. The deer circled while the wolves chased them, almost lazily, like sheepdogs herding a flock.

"Get on this side of the log and scrunch down," Jack said softly to Ashley, pulling her belt until she toppled backward, almost on top of him. "Keep your head low," he told her.

"I want to see!"

"You can see—just stay down. And keep quiet!"

The young deer hurtled across the meadow toward the steep hillside, changing direction as the two wolves bounded after it, separating it from the rest of the small herd. The wolves seemed to be playing with the deer, trying to scare it rather than zeroing in for a kill.

"I wish I had my binoculars," Ashley whispered.

"I've got mine," Jack murmured. "But you couldn't spot them—they're running too fast."

With the wolves in pursuit, the young mule deer doubled back to race across the meadow, heading for the creek. Suddenly the black wolf broke away to chase the four adult deer once again as they sprinted around the trampled grass. Only the gray wolf kept after the young deer, which crashed into the creek, its eyes wide and white with fear.

The deer was heading straight toward where Jack, Troy, and Ashley crouched behind the log, as if humans—even three of them—were less threatening than one large wolf.

Jack picked up his camera. "Don't move a muscle," he whispered to Ashley.

It took only seconds for the young deer to explode into the brush above the bank, right next to them. Jack tried to fire off a few pictures, but it was like trying to photograph lightning—the deer was just too swift.

Across the creek, the gray wolf stopped at the bank. After stepping gingerly into the shallow ripples that edged the creek, it paused and looked around. It almost seemed to be considering whether to follow the deer and get wet, or to forget the whole adventure and stay dry.

"Wow!" Jack whispered softly. "Look at him!"

The big wolf stood less than 40 feet from them. A black leather radio collar showed through the ruff of fur around his neck.

This was a young but full-grown male, a hundred-plus pounds of powerful muscle and thick gray fur.

Carefully, holding his breath, Jack raised his camera. At that slight motion the wolf snapped to attention, bouncing backward in surprise. For a brief moment the animal stood stiff-legged, staring straight at Jack, its yellow eyes gleaming. Then he pivoted and ran back across the meadow toward the rising hills. Loping halfway up the hill, he stopped, threw one brief, scornful glance toward Jack, and turned his attention to the other wolf, the black one, still running after the herd of deer.

Troy breathed, "That was—that was—"

He didn't finish saying what it was, but Jack understood, even though he couldn't have put words to it either. Nothing could adequately describe the thrill of seeing what they'd just seen, of being close enough that they'd actually been a part of it.

"Please, Jack, let me have your binoculars," Ashley begged. "He's standing still now and I want to get a good look."

"Okay," Jack agreed.

Right then he was feeling so good he would have given just about anything to just about anyone. Elation filled him, because he knew he'd clicked the shutter at just the right second. Not only once, but three times. Three pictures that should turn out to be outstanding, of the gray wolf staring right into the camera with those intense yellow eyes.

Jack couldn't wait to get home to his father's darkroom. Not that he'd develop the film himself—the negatives were too precious to take chances with. He'd ask his father for help.

"I can't see anything," Ashley complained as she swung the binoculars from side to side. "Yes, I do. Now I see something. A shirt."

"A shirt?" Troy asked in disbelief.

Just then the gray wolf raised his muzzle high, stretched his neck, and howled—once, twice, three times—calling for his mate.

Before the last howl faded, a shot rang out. The wolf leaped into the air and arced forward as if to run, but when his front paws hit the ground, his legs buckled and he fell.

"What! Jack!" Ashley screamed.

Too horrified even to yell, Jack gasped as the animal struggled to his feet, staggered for a moment, and then limped awkwardly toward the shelter of the trees.

"Get down, you moron! That was a gun!" Troy shouted. He grabbed Jack by the back of the neck and pushed his face into the dirt. At the same time he tackled Ashley around the knees, knocking her to the ground.

"Quit it!" Jack sputtered. "Let me up!"

"Someone's shooting. Do you want to get hit?"

"He shot the wolf!" Ashley shrieked. "There he is! Get his picture, Jack."

Jack scrambled up and clicked the shutter a couple of times, but it was useless. The gunman was too far away—at least a quarter of a mile—and camouflaged by branches and shadows.

"No good. He's gone," Jack said.

Because he was still peering through the lens, it took him several seconds to notice Troy climbing down toward the bank. Not till Jack heard splashes did he realize what was happening.

"Hey! Where do you think you're going?" he hollered.

Not even turning around, Troy answered, "The wolf's hurt. I'm gonna find it." Holding out his arms for balance, he skidded and slipped on the mossy rocks as he crossed the creek.

CHAPTER FOUR

Get back here now!" Jack screamed. Ashley's eyes flashed with fear.

Troy's sneakers, with no tread left, couldn't get enough traction on the algae-covered rocks. He slid awkwardly and landed with both feet on the creek bottom. For a few seconds he wobbled, but he managed to stay upright, even though his jeans got soaked all the way up to the hips.

"Troy!" Jack yelled. "Come back!"

He might as well have saved his breath. By then Troy had reached the opposite bank and was clambering over the rocks that lined the creek. Once he gained dry ground, he turned and flipped a nasty hand gesture at Jack.

Then he began to run across the meadow toward the steep incline of the foothills, heading to where the wolf's last howl had been cut short by gunfire.

"Jeez!" Jack cried, furious. "Now what am I supposed to do?"

"Go after him," Ashley said decidedly.

"OK. I guess I have to. You run back to the parking area and see if that ranger ever got there. Tell her what happened. Tell her to radio park headquarters for help."

So he wouldn't have to carry it, Jack pulled on his parka and again slid both arms through both straps of his backpack. His boots had been coated with water repellent, but even so, creek water seeped in through the laces and eyelets as he threaded his way across the creek, trying not to slip. If he fell in when Troy hadn't, humiliation would add fuel to his anger, which was already nearly hot enough to choke him. He glanced back only once to check on Ashley; she'd put on her own parka and was zipping it up.

Jack climbed as fast as he could. The higher he climbed the harder his breath came until at last it exploded from his lungs—not from exertion, but from fright. He'd begun to wonder what he was walking into. The more he thought about it, the more scared he got.

There was a guy with a gun up there!

He could be anywhere! Maybe right that minute he was hiding in the pines with a high-powered rifle raised to his shoulder, pointed at Jack. In his mind's eye, Jack could picture a man, squinting into the rifle scope, his finger on the trigger....

A pebble rolled downhill. Panic bored into Jack's

brain like a bullet. Whirling around, he searched the trees; was that the glint of a rifle barrel over by that rock? Or the shape of a man melting into those tree shadows on the right? With each step his fear mounted higher and gripped him tighter until he threw himself flat onto the ground and covered his head with his arms.

Lying there, he realized that his purple parka must stand out like a flashing beacon against the autumn-yellowed grass, so conspicuous that only a blind person could possibly miss it. His heart pounded. Was it better to get up and run, to lie still and keep a low profile, or to crawl for cover?

What cover? He was in an open area with no trees or brush or boulders nearby. Facedown, he stayed motionless until his heart slowed a little and he could hear more than the blood pumping around his ears. Wind pushed through the trees, making them shudder. Another gust of wind; it ruffled his hair like fingers. Then silence. Cautiously, he lifted his head and pushed himself to his knees.

As he did, on the ground next to him he saw the blood—bright, vivid red on the flattened grass where he'd been lying.

He raised his hands; a small amount of blood smeared one palm. He rubbed it against his jeans.

That must have been where the wolf fell before it struggled up again. Leaning forward on hands and knees, Jack stared down, trying to judge just how much blood had been spilled. As much as a cupful? More? How much blood could a wolf lose before it dropped, too weak to go on? Maybe the wolf wouldn't get too far. Troy must be following the trail of blood, and wherever it ended, when the wolf finally weakened and dropped, Jack would probably find both of them.

"Hi!"

"WHA—" Jack's heart lurched wildly into his throat; he couldn't even shriek. Caught totally off guard, he jerked so hard his teeth rattled.

"What are you doing on the ground like that?" Ashley asked him. "I've been watching you. First you were flat on your belly, now you're on all fours. You're acting really weird, Jack."

Scrambling to his feet, Jack drilled his finger into her chest and yelled, "So just what the crud are you doing up here, sneaking up on me like that and scaring me to death? I told you to go back and get the ranger. You turn yourself right around and head down that hill. Now!"

"Forget it," Ashley said.

"Forget it?" Jerking his fingers through his hair, Jack seethed. No matter how hard he tried to make people do what they were supposed to, they kept running straight through him as though he were nothing more than a ghost.

"Why didn't you listen to me?" he shouted. "Now I might never be able to find Troy. You didn't get help like you were supposed to and you're costing me all this time—you've got to go back and tell the ranger what's happening. I mean it, Ashley!"

She stared right back at him. "You're not the boss of me, Jack, even if you think you are. I want to help find Troy, too. Besides, you need me."

"Need you?" Jack cried. "What do I need you for?"

Ashley crossed her arms. "To help track him, that's what. I read about it in a book, so I know how to do it."

Jack leaned as close to her face as he could. "You read a book! Wow! So now you're an expert."

"No, but—"

"Ashley, listen to me. If Troy makes it to a road, he can hitch a ride and disappear, and then Mom and Dad'll be screwed. Don't you get it? This is real serious trouble, Ashley. Big time."

"You're right. Troy's getting away, and we're wasting time. That means we better get started."

"Go back!" he thundered.

Anger began to spark behind Ashley's eyes. Jack knew how easygoing his sister was, how she usually let everyone else have their way while she tried to keep things smooth. But when Ashley was pushed, she could flare like a rocket. Now, leaning forward, fists tight, she pulled herself as tall as she could. "You don't ever give me a chance. At home you're always telling me what to do. I'm sick of it."

Jack argued, "I'm the one who's responsible for you

and Troy! I don't even know if I can find him now. I don't know if he'll come with me when I do."

"Why should he? You've been mad at him ever since he showed up at our house."

That stopped Jack cold. It took him a moment to stutter, "I have not been mad. When did I ever say anything?"

"Yeah, right." Ashley had been standing downhill; now she moved around to the uphill side of Jack so their heads were even and their eyes were level. "Even if you don't say things out loud, people still know what you're thinking. Your face gets all scrunched up and you walk away and hide in your room. Troy's not stupid. He's had bad stuff happen to him, and he's all alone and you haven't made it one bit better. He won't listen to you, but he might listen to me."

For a moment, neither one of them spoke. Ashley's breath came in little gasps, but her face stayed set and defiant. She was right, and Jack knew it.

"So do you want to keep yelling, or do you want us to go find Troy?" she asked.

Jack knew when he was defeated, but there was no law that said he had to give in gracefully. "Okay, fine. Since you're so smart," he growled, "where should we start?"

"Over there, in the trees."

"Any particular trees?" he asked sarcastically.

"Yes. Those particular trees." Sounding just as flip, she jerked her thumb to the right. "I was watching Troy when he ran. In this book I read about tracking animals and people, it said to always pick out a landmark where you saw them last. See that big rock up there?" She pointed. "It's right next to a tree that's all brown and has one branch drooping all the way down to the ground—like maybe it was hit by lightning. That's where Troy went. I paid attention, when I saw him go, and I picked out that landmark. He ran right between the rock and that tree."

Jack just stared at her.

"Once we get there," she went on, "it'll be easy to follow his footprints. His shoes were soaked, remember? He's leaving wet tracks."

Jack took a deep breath. It was time, now, to yield as gracefully as he could manage since his sister was making a lot of sense. "Okay. The sun's already down to the tops of the trees. We don't have much time. So let's go."

"You go first," Ashley said, giving him one of her big, generous smiles, because she'd won.

Even if she was his sister, Jack had to admit that Ashley was pretty smart. Just as she'd predicted, when they reached the rock next to the hanging branch, they saw that dampness had squeezed down from Troy's dripping jeans and waterlogged sneakers to mark his path. That wouldn't last too long, Jack knew. In the thin mountain air, Troy's clothes would soon dry out— they'd stop leaving damp traces in the dust. And as the sun kept sinking lower, shadows would begin to hide the wolf's blood spots that Troy must have been following: bright red drops would fade in the darkness, becoming almost invisible to the eye.

As if reading Jack's thoughts, Ashley said, "We'll look for bent grass and twigs. And places where stones were kicked out of the way—that's what the book said to do."

Once they'd entered the gloom of the trees, Jack found himself lowering his voice to speak more softly. He still felt the prickly sensation that the man with the gun might be hiding in the shadows, stalking them. Baldheads, that Minnesota woman had called them, but that wasn't the real name. They dressed in black leather and wore high, shiny black boots and armbands, and shaved their heads to make themselves look even meaner. Jack shuddered. He sure didn't want to meet up with one of them in these woods. Twice, he made Ashley stand stock still, so he could listen hard for any unusual sounds, but except for the rustling of branches in the breeze, all was quiet.

"It can't be too hard to track things up here," Ashley was saying. "Mom talked about how they're always tracking wolves, right?"

"That's different. They do that with antennas that pick up radio signals from the wolves' collars."

"Like the antenna on our jeep?"

"Mmmmm, sort of," he answered. "Except they look more like small TV antennas, the kind we have on our roof at home, only miniature. The rangers carry them around and lift them up—" Jack raised his arm to demonstrate. "Or else they fly over the park in airplanes and use special receivers to listen for radio signals."

"Oh." Ashley managed, easily, to keep up with Jack. She stayed right at his back and she wasn't even breathing hard, although they'd been moving pretty fast for about half a mile. "So how does it work?" she asked. "How can they tell where the wolves are?"

"Well, it's like—" Jack thought hard, trying to remember what he'd overheard when his parents talked about wolf tracking. "Each wolf's radio collar has its own frequency. It's like a special code. You know how when you turn on our car radio, each radio station has a number? They're all broadcasting different stuff, music or sports or news, from different places, but you can tune in lots of stations by moving the dial to the different numbers. So when rangers pick up a signal on their receiving antenna, they can tell which wolf it's coming from and where the wolf is. Get it?"

"Uh...huh," Ashley said uncertainly.

"Anyway, stop asking questions now and keep watching for the blood drops."

After a while the trees thinned out and they came to a mound of gray granite rock. Two and a half billion years earlier, the earth had convulsed and heaved up a massive mountain range in what was now Yellowstone. Over eons, from wind and weather, the rough mountains wore down. At the same time living things grew and then died, so that each season added layer upon thin layer of new soil. Year after year roots worked into cracks, grinding the granite into dust that became deep enough, over time, to nurture tall trees. Yet in other places like this one the bare rock remained, great slabs of it, rigid and unmoving, waiting for the earth to shudder in its next upheaval.

It would take Jack and Ashley too long to hike to the top of the mound of rock or to circle around it at the bottom, so Jack started across it, balancing easily, leaping across clefts and fissures. As the low sun bathed the mound with a warm yellow glow, he noticed three blood spots, about six inches apart, all in a line. He felt a surge of excitement. They were on the right track!

Behind him, Ashley clambered over the rocks like a mountain goat. "If I was a wolf, I'd hate to wear a collar. I bet they try to get them off. Jack, did you ever see those pictures of coyotes wearing bandannas around their necks? That's so dumb, because a real coyote could chew off a bandanna in about ten seconds—"

"Quiet!" Jack held up his hand. By then they'd reached the next patch of forest. Once more he strained to hear whether anyone was following them, although the farther they went, the less threatened he felt.

They stood in the near darkness, breathing softly. The pines seemed to sigh, but all else was still.

Suddenly, in the distance, they heard a howl. Wolf

song! Was it the wounded wolf crying out? Then there were more howls. Jack tried to separate them, to count how many wolves might be out there, but one call would barely die away before the next one began.

Other wolves took up the song, yipping and howling, almost in harmony. Perhaps they were serenading the dying sun, or maybe they were talking, in wolf language, about their brother wolf who'd been shot.

They sounded nearby. His parents had told him that on the entire North American continent, no human being had ever been harmed by a healthy wolf. "Rabid wolves?—yes, maybe," his mother had said. "Captive wolves?—that's another story. Wolves were never meant to live in captivity. But no healthy wolf in the wild in North America has ever killed a person." Still....Jack shivered as the howls seemed to surround them.

Ashley grabbed his arm and looked at him with eyes brimming with wonder. Her smile lit her whole face. "We're so lucky!" she whispered.

"Yeah." He whispered, too, and smiled back at her, knowing how right she was. For that magic moment they were lucky, to stand in the stillness of the wilderness, listening to wolf song the way few people were ever privileged to hear it.

The sun set behind the mountain, and almost unbelievably soon, they found themselves in a gray, dusky world where a rock might be an animal, or a lost boy. Or where a tree might be a man with a gun.

How were they ever going to follow Troy's tracks now, Jack wondered. As he hesitated, the answer reached him—in fact, it fell on him. First one snowflake, then a dozen, then enough gentle flakes to make the faintest skiff of white on the ground, and to glisten in Ashley's dark hair.

"Pull your hood up," he told her. "We have to move really fast while this twilight lasts so we can follow Troy's footprints in the snow."

It worked for a little while. Forging ahead, they did discover Troy's footprints, and were able to track them along a twisting trail, over bare rock and through brush and trees.

Then darkness fell completely.

CHAPTER FIVE

Even a candle would have given more light than the two-and-a-half-inch, squeeze-till-it-lights-up flashlight that was meant to hang from a key chain and target a door lock at night. But that was all they had. On the snow-dusted forest floor, its feeble light got swallowed like a firefly inside a whale.

"I wish we had a real flashlight," Ashley said. "That one sure is little."

"Better than nothing," Jack told her. At least it let him avoid any low branches that might have smacked him in the face, or any big rocks he might have tripped over.

Harder to see were Troy's footprints. Although the snow was falling only lightly, it had begun to fill in the tracks left by Troy and the wolf. Any blood drops were now totally impossible to find. And Jack was getting cold and hungry.

"We're gonna have to give it up," he sighed.

"Why? Are you tired?"

"Who, me? No—I was worried about you." Turning around, he shone the flashlight right into her face, but it was such a puny little light that she didn't even blink. "There's no way we can find our way back the way we came, but we don't need to," he said. "If we just keep walking down the mountain, we'll get to Slough Creek sooner or later. Then we can follow the creek to the parking lot and someone will be there to take us to park headquarters. They've probably got a whole rescue squad out by now."

Ashley sat down on a fallen tree and leaned her crossed arms on her knees. "That's good for us. But what about Troy?"

"What about him? We tried. We did our best, but it didn't work. He'll be OK. The biggest problem for Troy is that it's going to get really cold here tonight—"

"And we have our parkas, but Troy only has that jacket of his," she said. "He's going to freeze. And I bet he doesn't know that if he goes down the hill he'll get to Slough Creek, 'cause he doesn't know squat about wilderness. Which means we've got to find him."

"What do you think we've been trying to do? What else is there?"

"We'll yell," she announced.

"Ashley, he'll never hear."

"He will if we yell loud enough. TROY! TROY! Where are you? Can you hear me?"

In the cold, crisp air, sound traveled much more clearly than they would have expected. Although there was no telling how far away it might be, Jack and Ashley heard a faint, "Yeah, I hear you."

Ashley scrambled to her feet. "KEEP YELLING, TROY! Come on," she said to Jack, "he's up the hill that way."

"No, wait a second," Jack argued. "I think the sound's coming from the other way."

"Hey, Troy!" Ashley called. "Say something again!" Without waiting for Jack, she fought through brush to climb a steep incline. "Holler something, Troy!"

The answering call sounded a little closer. "SHUT UP!"

Ashley laughed. "That's Troy, all right."

She climbed in a nearly straight line. If a tree got in her way, she circled around it, and then got right back onto her arrow-straight path, jumping over fallen branches, kicking aside rocks, pushing through ground cover. How could she be so sure where she was headed, Jack wondered—in the dark, and even after Troy stopped answering their calls?

He shook his head in amazement, when, within 15 minutes, she'd found him.

Troy was hunched over the wolf's unmoving body, his hands hovering above it as though he could press some of his own life into the wolf by sheer will. Scarcely visible in the dim light from Jack's little flashlight, blood oozed through the wolf's thick, silver fur, melting into the earth.

"Wait—Troy—get away from him!" Jack cried. "You don't know anything about wild animals. He'll bite your hand off!"

The wolf's yellow eyes fluttered open, then closed, like butterfly wings.

"He won't hurt me," Troy muttered. "He knows I want to help."

"Yeah, right," Jack answered. "That's just what he'll say to himself when he crunches down on your arm. You can't help the wolf, Troy. The only thing we can do for him is go back right now and tell people where he is. They'll come get him first thing in the morning."

"In the morning he'll be dead," Troy said.

"Nuh-UH!" Ashley shook her head vehemently.

Jack thought the chances of the wolf lasting through the night were pretty slim, but he had to get Troy out of there.

"He'll make it," Jack said. "He's got a radio collar on. The rangers'll follow the signal and...."

"Shine your light here," Troy said, pointing to the rectangular box at the bottom of the wolf's collar, the part that held the batteries.

"Yeah?" Jack peered more closely. "What?"

"Just look. See that?" The battery pack was shattered as if something inside it had exploded.

"What happened to it?"

"Some jerk shot it," Troy said. "A piece of the bullet's still jammed inside there—you can see it."

"I don't get it. If it tore up the collar, how can he be bleeding from his side?" Jack asked. It didn't make sense. "I mean, it couldn't have hit him in his left side and then gone around the front to smash into the collar, could it?"

"No. I've seen gunshot wounds before," Troy said. "The torn place in his side's from a bullet. One hit there, and another one got the collar."

"But there was only one shot," Ashley insisted. "Right, Jack? You heard it same as me. It was so loud we couldn't have missed it if there'd been a second one."

"Don't worry about it now," Jack said. "We need to get moving. Come on, Troy. It's late, and it's going to be a long hike down to the creek."

For a moment Troy didn't answer. Then he said, "If the wolf dies, I don't want him to die alone. I'm staying."

"Are you crazy? What good will that do?" Jack started to protest, but Ashley pulled on his hand to quiet him as Troy knelt closer to the wolf.

The big animal really did appear near death. Its mouth opened, letting the tongue loll out as if the wolf needed more air, yet its chest barely moved. Speaking very softly, Troy said, "He's scared. I want to be here for him."

"It would be hard to find our way in the dark, Jack," Ashley murmured.

Jack must have been getting tired, or maybe even

colder, because his brain stopped working normally: suddenly everything Troy and Ashley were saying seemed not only reasonable, but...the only right thing to do. "Okay," he sighed. "We'll stay here."

Troy just grunted, "Up to you."

"So the first thing we need," Jack decided, "is a fire. Not just to stay warm. Everyone will be out looking for us—if they spot a fire, they'll get here quicker. You go pick up some firewood, Ashley," he ordered. "Get plenty, and make sure it's dry. Go on— what are you waiting for? Go do it right now while I find a good place to build the fire."

"Did you bring matches?" Ashley asked.

"What do you think?"

"Of course. 'Cause you're so perfect, aren't you, Jack?"

"What's that supposed to mean?" Jack demanded.

"Nothing. Just that you're the bossiest brother in the whole state of Wyoming, that's all. Don't you ever get tired telling people what to do?"

He choked off the next words he would have added if Troy hadn't been there: that he took charge because he was better than anyone else at getting things done. Especially in the situation they were in right then. "I'm not bossy," he told Ashley. "I'm...responsible."

"Responsible. That's supposed to be good, huh?" Ashley picked up a long, thin pine branch and cracked it hard over her bent leg, breaking it in two. "So if it's so great, why don't you ever give anyone else a chance to be responsible?"

"Okay!" he yelled. "I'll give you a chance. What do you want to be responsible for?"

Ashley appeared to be thinking it over.

"We need some dry tinder to start the fire," she answered. "I'll go find it."

"That's what I told you in the first place!"

"But now...I'm telling myself." Head high, she walked off, leaving Jack muttering.

The forest was damp, but Ashley knew what to do. She felt along the base of a tree where pine needles had piled up around the trunk; in spite of the thin layer of snow, the ones underneath were still dry.

"Bring me the light, OK?" she called to Jack. While Jack used brush to clear a patch of ground, Ashley hunted for a fallen tree. When she found one, she shone the light inside the hollow, dried-out trunk to make sure no sharp-toothed rodents or unfriendly snakes were in residence. All was clear, so she reached in to pull out loose bits of splintered dry wood.

While Jack lit the pine needles and wood bits, Ashley pulled bark and twigs from the dry underside of the fallen tree, then picked up larger branches that had broken off when the tree fell, probably years before. Within ten minutes they had a small, bright fire. Once it was going, Jack and Ashley fed larger branches into it, before dragging rocks into a circle around the blaze.

"Leave that end open," Jack instructed Ashley. "I want the heat to reach out toward the wolf."

"Bossy," Ashley said under her breath, but she did what Jack told her.

Although Troy hung over the wolf and mostly just kept staring at it, from time to time he shot sideways glances at Jack and Ashley, listening to their verbal sparring and watching them work on the fire.

Now, silence hung over them, except for the crackling of the fire. The quietness pressed down like the few lazy flakes of snow that had just about stopped falling. Ashley felt it too, because she got over being mad and started to chatter the way she always did when conversation stopped too long to suit her.

"You built an Indian fire, Jack, not a white-man's fire. An Indian cooks his food, but a white man cooks himself." She'd heard their parents say that on almost every camping trip.

"Food!" Jack said. "I forgot I have half a box of those Ritz peanut-butter crackers in my backpack. I'm starving!"

"Me, too," Ashley agreed. When Jack produced the box she reached inside it, pulled out a cracker, and munched greedily.

Walking over to where Troy crouched, Jack said, "You want some?"

"Sure. OK." Troy held out his hand, and Jack put a few crackers into his upraised palm. As their hands touched, Jack realized how cold Troy's felt.

"Are your shoes still wet?" he asked.

"Yeah. It doesn't matter," Troy answered with his mouth full.

"Sure it does! Take them off, and your socks, too, and dry them by the fire. I mean, if you want to. I have an extra pair of socks in my backpack."

"You're a regular Boy Scout, right?" Troy said. "Like, be prepared—you know?"

That was halfway between a compliment and a put-down, but Jack didn't care. "Yeah, actually, I am," he answered. He tossed the socks to Troy, who caught them with one hand.

"Jack's working on Eagle Scout," Ashley bragged. "But the reason he has the socks is because Mom always makes us carry an extra pair in our camping packs." Suddenly, Ashley's voice wavered and her shoulders slumped. "I wonder where Mom is. Shouldn't they be coming down off the mountain by now? I wish they'd find us, Jack. It's kind of scary up here."

Jack put his arm around her and said, "It'll be OK. Nothing bad's going to happen to us." Awkwardly, he patted her shoulder through the padding of her down-filled parka.

Troy watched, no longer stealing glances but staring straight at them. He seemed puzzled by the way they acted with one another. Jack guessed that for an only kid like Troy, it must be confusing to hear a brother and sister argue half the time and then see them hug like they cared about each other. Which they did. As Troy struggled to pull on the dry socks, he seemed to be working his way a little closer to the fire, inch by inch.

Suddenly, Ashley stiffened. "What was that!" she demanded, sitting up straight.

"What?"

"That thing that was moving around in those trees. Over there!"

"Where?" Jack squinted.

He held up his hand to shield his eyes from the fire until his sight could adjust to the darkness, but he didn't see anything. The earlier fears stabbed him again, of the man who'd shot the wolf and of his powerful rifle. "Troy," Jack said quietly, "come with me to check it out, OK?"

"No. It's just trees."

"But I saw it. There was a black shape moving around over that way," Ashley insisted, pointing. She didn't take her eyes off the patch of forest directly in front of them.

Troy just shook his head.

"If my sister says she saw something, then she saw something," Jack told Troy. "At least you could help me look."

"You're the man with the light. You go check it out."

So that was how it was still going to be. No matter how many chances Jack gave him, Troy always ended up being a jerk.

"Want me to go with you, Jack?" Ashley asked.

"No, you stay here." No use both of us getting killed, he added silently. Acting a lot braver than he felt, he squeezed the pitifully small light and moved toward the trees Ashley had pointed to. He heard a sound like the whisper of a breeze. Maybe Troy was right, and it was only tree limbs rustling. But that didn't stop the pulse from pounding in Jack's neck.

Behind him, Ashley's voice was cautious. "Can you see anything?"

"Not yet." Peering into the inky blackness, he took another step. Branches cracked underneath his feet but beyond that sound, he thought he heard the faintest scratching in the darkness. Then, once again, stillness.

"What is it?" she asked, louder this time.

Jack shook his head. "It could have been shadows from the fire," he answered, hoping he was right. "Whatever it was, it's gone now."

"Told you," Troy sneered.

"Yeah, well, thanks for the help."

Pinching the top of his coat, Jack came back to the fire, dropped down, and leaned toward the flames until one side of his face got too hot. Then he turned to warm his other side. Luckily, the cloud cover that had produced the few flakes of snow acted like a lid—it kept some of the day's warmth close to the earth, and held the night's cold at bay higher above. Still, Jack thought, Troy must be feeling the chill in his flimsy jacket. Served him right.

"Troy's got to be really cold," Ashley whispered, echoing Jack's thoughts.

"So?"

"So ask him to sit with us."

"After the way he blew us off? Let him freeze."

"Please, Jack? He'll come over if you ask."

Looking into her wide, dark eyes, Jack wondered at the way his sister could let slights and insults roll off her. Things bothered Jack a lot more. But...."Hey, Troy," he called. "You can't do any more for the wolf. Come sit by the fire."

"I want to stay with Silver."

"Silver?"

"That's his name."

"Who decided?"

"Me."

Jack shrugged. "OK, so he's Silver. He'll be fine for a while. Come on over and get warm."

Troy didn't answer and didn't move. Oh well, Jack thought. But Ashley, rising to her feet, walked toward Troy's dark shape and put her hand on his shoulder. There was no way Jack would ever think about touching Troy, and he half expected Troy to slap Ashley's hand away.

"I like the name Silver," she said. "It's a perfect wolf name."

Troy grunted.

But he didn't shake his shoulder free.

"You know what? I was thinking that maybe you're scaring Silver 'cause you're so close to him. Animals aren't used to people."

"He's used to me. I don't want him to think he's alone."

"He knows you're here." When Troy didn't respond, Ashley tried again. "I want to tell a story, but I can't unless we're by the fire—it's too cold over here. Come on and be with us, Troy."

Watching them, Jack understood that Ashley was gently nudging Troy, like water against soft sand. And just as suddenly, he realized how much it bothered him to see his sister try so hard to reach such a loser. Troy was hopeless—he cared only about himself and that wolf—and Jack didn't want Ashley getting put down by him.

"Ashley, come back here," Jack commanded.

"Hey—she's comin'." And then, to Jack's amazement, Troy unbent himself and followed Ashley to a spot spread with pine boughs, where he sat down next to her. When he held his hands to the flame, Jack saw how purple the tips of Troy's fingers had become. With a long stick, Jack stabbed the embers and stirred them.

"Let's hear the story," Troy said.

CHAPTER SIX

In the days before the ancient times, Sin-a-wavi the Wolf was the Creator. Back then, only Sin-a-wavi and his little brother, Coyote, lived on the Earth. They had come out of the light, so long ago that no one remembered when or how.

Because the Earth was so beautiful, it needed people to live on it. Sin-a-wavi gave a bag of sticks to his little brother, Coyote, and said, "Carry these over the far hills to the valley beyond."

He told Coyote how he must perform the task, and what he should do when he reached the valley. "This is a great responsibility," Sin-a-wavi said. "Do not open the bag! Not for any reason. Not until you come to the sacred ground in the valley."

"What is this that I must carry?" asked Coyote.

"I will say no more about it," Sin-a-wavi answered. "Go now, and do as I have told you."

Coyote was young and foolish, and full of curiosity. "What is this that I am carrying?" he kept asking himself. As soon as he was over the first hill and out of sight, he stopped. He thought he might just peek into the bag. "That couldn't hurt anything," Coyote said to himself.

He untied the top of the bag and opened it just a little bit. Suddenly, creatures rushed to the opening. They were people! They jumped out and ran every which way, yelling and hollering in all kinds of languages.

Coyote tried to grab them and stuff them back into the bag, but there were too many of them, and they ran too fast.

From the feel of the bag when he got it closed again, Coyote could tell there were only a few of what he started out with left. He went to the sacred valley and dumped them out there. Then he returned and told Sin-a-wavi that he'd completed the task he was given.

Sin-a-wavi searched Coyote's face. "I see the truth," he said. "Foolish little brother! You do not know what a fearful thing you've done."

"I tried to catch them!" Coyote confessed. "I was frightened! They spoke in strange tongues that I couldn't understand."

Sin-a-wavi said, "Those you let escape will forever be at war with the chosen ones, the Utes. The Utes, even though they are few, will be the mightiest and most valiant of heart. As for the other tribes, they will forever be thorns in their sides."

Sin-a-wavi, the Wolf, then put this curse on Coyote: "You irresponsible meddler! From now on you will be doomed to wander the Earth at night. On all fours."

"But then," Ashley added in her usual voice, "the coyote and the wolf became really good friends and they stopped arguing."

"I think maybe you made that last part up," Troy said. "But it was a good story. I liked it. 'Cause the wolf was the boss of everything."

"I heard it from a Ute Indian storyteller. I tried to say it just like he did, but he sounded better."

"You did good," Troy told her.

It was late, close to ten by the big digital numbers on the watch that circled Troy's bony wrist. Ashley yawned a wide, gulping yawn.

Stretching his arms over his head, Jack said, "OK, it's time to shut down for the night. Ashley, you need to go to sleep right now."

"Not yet," she said. A little smile lifted the corners of her mouth. "I want Troy to tell a story."

"Come on, he's not going to know any campfire stories. Right, Troy?"

Troy looked up sharply, but remained silent. The fire licked the darkness with orange tongues that darted this way and that. Ashley, too, shifted from side to side, trying to find a comfortable spot.

"Ashley—" Jack began again.

"Yeah, I'll tell you a story," Troy broke in. "A real-life mystery. It's about the last time I heard from my mom."

Pine sap snapped in the flames as Ashley leaned forward, fixing her gaze on Troy's face as he began softly, "The last time I heard her voice, she called me on the phone." His eyes didn't move off the blue-edged flames. Ashley nodded, encouraging him to go on.

"She was at work, and she said she'd had a really bad day and she wanted to get out of that bar and all the smoke and get to some clean air. She said she'd be late 'cause she was picking up stuff on her way home from work. 'Don't eat anything,' she said, 'Tonight we're havin' hot dogs.' So I waited and waited. I got hungry, but I didn't eat—didn't even drink a soda pop. The clock in our kitchen ticks real loud, and by nine o'clock I wanted to throw that thing across the room. It was raining, real hard. Every time the lightning hit, I looked out my window, up and down our street, hoping I'd see something. She never came."

"Maybe...I mean, do you think she went to a friend's house?" Jack suggested.

"Yeah, right," Troy snapped. "She's off at a friend's and doesn't even think to call me, not for all these days. Get real! Anyway, we don't have any friends. You don't get to know people when you move around like we do."

"How come you move so much?" Ashley had a way

of asking things so innocently that people never felt she was prying.

"I don't know." Troy shrugged. "My mom's always saying we're part gypsy. Anyway, I like living the way we do, just the two of us and nobody else. I've stood inside half the bars and bowling alleys between here and New York while I waited for my mom to get off work. Most of 'em were dumps, but some were sort of OK."

Ashley asked, "Weren't you ever scared?"

"Of what? I've seen guns and knives and drunken fights—up to now, nothing's hurt us. My mom's tough. We do what we want and we live how we want. No one tells us what to do."

Suddenly Jack hit on a possibility. Without thinking, he blurted, "Your dad! What about your dad? Did you tell him your mom's gone? I mean, maybe she went there, to be where he is."

"My dad?"

"Do you...I mean—"

Snorting, Troy said, "Yeah, I've got one, but I haven't seen him in so long I can't hardly remember. It's weird. The only real memory I have of him is his black leather jacket."

"His jacket?" Ashley repeated.

"Yeah. He used to wear this really cool bomber one, you know, the kind bikers wear? My mom said that in our neighborhood, somebody'd probably kill him just for what he put on his back." Troy slid his fingers through his hair, dividing it into dark strings. "The day he left they were fighting about that jacket. My mom told him he had no right blowing $400 on a jacket like that, and he told her he needed something to protect his back 'cause she was always all over him, weighing him down so bad he could hardly move. So my mom said, 'If that's how you feel about Troy and me, why don't you just back yourself right out the door?' And he said, 'I'm out of here. But I'm taking the kid.'"

It seemed to Jack as if even the wind got quiet. "So what happened?" he asked.

Troy stared into the fire. "My mom pulled out a kitchen knife. She told him that if he wanted me, he'd have to get by her first. She said nothing in the whole world was as important to her as I was. So he left. I've never seen him since."

"How old were you?" It was Ashley, her voice only a murmur.

"Me? I don't know." He counted back, a faraway look in his eyes.

"I guess I was sev—no, almost eight."

Jack's thoughts recoiled at the image of a seven-year-old boy watching his mom threaten his dad with a knife. He'd never experienced anything remotely like what Troy had just described. Ashley shouldn't be hearing stories like these—she didn't need to have her mind rubbed into that kind of ugliness. It was time to close her off from Troy.

"Hey, guys, it's getting late." Jack rubbed the back of his neck, hardly feeling the sensation because he'd grown so cold. "Ashley, you need to go to sleep. If searchers don't find us tonight, we'll have to get up at dawn and start down the hill."

He sounded bossy even to himself, but for some reason Jack couldn't shut it off. "Try to get your feet next to the flames so they won't freeze, but not so close that you might roll in. And pull the string of your hood as tight as it will go."

Troy hunkered himself up. The light caught on the zippers of the bomber jacket and made them shine with a diamond hardness. Narrowing his eyes, he said, "Wait a minute. I was talkin' here. You know, your sister's right, man—you're a real dictator. What gives you the right?"

The question took Jack by surprise; he felt the heat rise to his cheeks as he stumbled for an answer. "Because—I'm...older."

Ashley was staring at him, he could feel it, but he didn't pull his eyes off Troy's.

"Not older than me. I've got a whole year on you that says Ashley can stay up as long as she wants."

Jack swallowed. "No, she can't. I'm in charge. Not you."

"You're—in—charge?" Troy drew out the words. "Why? Just 'cause you don't like me and you don't like hearing about my life? I saw the way your face got all twisted when I was talking about my dad. You think I'm stupid?"

"You really want me to answer that?" It was a risky thing to say, but Jack was sick of Troy's tough attitude.

Rising to his feet, Troy took a step. "Oh, so you think you're better than me, right? You think since you got two parents and a house—you can get over on me 'cause you think me and my mom are just trailer trash. Is that it?"

"Give me a break," Jack said hotly. "If I don't like you it's because you're a jerk. You blow off me and Ashley—in fact, my whole family! You do whatever you want even if it's wrong—"

"Wrong? I've been wrong?" Troy's voice shot up.

"Yeah." Now Jack jumped to his feet and stood, poker straight. "Like you take off after a wolf and get us all in trouble."

"Jack—" Ashley tried to break in, but he waved her off. The battle was between him and Troy. "My parents are probably freaking out right now—"

Troy sliced the air with his hand. "No one said you had to come with me."

"Right. I let you go, and you find a highway and hitch a ride back—"

"So?"

"So what about my folks? They're responsible for you—"

"Oh, man, more of that responsibility crap! So someone in Social Services gets a little ticked and your parents get their hands slapped—I don't care. I was trying to save the wolf's life! Besides, I got bigger problems," Troy raged.

"Why is it your problem? You didn't shoot that wolf!"

"It's not the wolf! Doesn't anybody get it? My—mom—is—gone!" His hand made a fist.

Jack noticed but it didn't matter. He lifted his chin; Troy did the same. The hair prickled on Jack's head as he waited for the next words, the next move.

"Troy...what happened with your mom...it's not Jack's fault." Ashley's voice, steady and calm, worked its way between them. "It's not my fault, and it's not my mom's or dad's—it's not anybody's fault. It just happened. And Troy, it's not your fault."

The last words seemed to hit Troy right in the gut. A gust of air escaped his lips. The wind blew colder, but he stood rigid, not wanting to make the first move. Slowly, his fist drifted to his side. "I—I didn't..." He couldn't finish. Just then, an eerie howl split the night air, lonesome and empty as a train song. Less than 15 feet away a dark shape darted through the trees, melting into one shadow, then another. A rustling, and then a streak of black. The campfire cast enough light for Jack to see two gold-green eyes reflecting in the darkness.

"Troy—Jack," Ashley breathed. "Look! Look at Silver!"

The wolf's head had raised almost six inches from the earth, hovering for a moment, straining toward the shape beyond, before sinking back into the ground.

"Over there," Jack whispered, pointing to a cluster of fir trees. "I bet it's Silver's mate. That must have been what you saw before, Ashley. She was out there all along, just watching him."

"You think so?" Ashley asked softly.

"Yeah—remember how there were two of them this morning? Wolves stay together for life. I bet she's going to watch over him all night."

"Hang tough, Silver," Troy murmured. "She's with you now. You're gonna make it. Just hang in there, boy."

He couldn't explain how it happened, but suddenly Jack realized that the wolf and Troy and Troy's mother had all meshed together somehow, and each piece told something about the other, just like Ashley's story. No wonder Troy had gone after the wolf. Troy had lived through violent times, same as Silver. Both had been wounded. Maybe it was just by a thread, but the two of them were hanging on.

Another thought worked its way through Jack's mind while they stood, straining to see in the darkness. There was no way Jack could have made it if he'd lived the life Troy had. And if he'd survived, he knew he would have come out of it as prickly as Troy. Maybe, Jack thought with a start, he might have turned out worse. Pulling his jacket tighter, he wondered if this was the reason his dad had decided to bring new people into their cozy world.

The wolf howled again.

"Will she hurt us?" Ashley asked.

"Nah. We just need to stay together." He hesitated, started to speak, stopped, then started again. "Come on, Troy."

Troy's eyes slid onto Jack's, wary.

"It's OK. We'll be safe by the fire."

Troy looked at Jack for what felt like a long time. "I need to watch Silver," he said. "I gotta make sure he doesn't get too cold."

"I'll keep moving the fire closer to him," Jack offered. "Every time I add wood, I'll string it out so it's nearer to him. OK?"

"No, I'll do it," Troy said. "You can sleep. I'll stay up all night."

"We'll take turns," Jack told him.

CHAPTER SEVEN

By three in the morning the protective cloud cover had moved away, leaving no barrier against the frigid temperatures that pressed down on the mountain. But it was not the cold that woke Jack.

In his sleep he'd moved nearer to the warmth of the fire, until his face got too close to the ashes and he coughed. Sitting up, he coughed again, and shook his head to clear away the buzzing.

The buzzing continued in his head, like a huge insect, until he suddenly realized that the loud humming was coming from overhead. Jack looked up and scrambled to his feet.

Red and white wing lights of a small airplane flashed alternately, a beacon in the night sky. The plane was circling slowly overhead.

It was all he could do not to cry out or wave his arms. That would be a useless waste of energy; he knew he needed to work fast and work smart. The fire was the only thing that an airplane could see, and right now it had burned low. With shaking hands, Jack quickly threw every piece of brush and tinder he could reach onto the embers. He even dumped on the empty Ritz cracker box, and watched it flare up and then blacken as the letters crumpled inward.

"What..." Troy mumbled, opening his eyes.

"Nothing. Just fixing the fire," Jack said. "Go back to sleep."

The flames rose satisfyingly high while the plane still circled. They'll see it, Jack thought. They can't miss it. As he watched the light aircraft fly, he moved closer to the fire to warm his cold hands. Troy, who'd been shivering and hugging himself tightly, relaxed a little as more heat reached him. Let them sleep, Jack thought. Why wake Troy and Ashley and get them all excited? If that pilot is searching for us, he's seen the fire. Otherwise...Plan B. We hike out in the morning.

In a few minutes the plane flew away—in a straight line. That was a good sign. It meant the pilot had decided he didn't need to search any longer. He was probably already radioing the location to park headquarters, where the rescue team would be packing up to start their trek. More than likely, though, they'd wait for the first bit of daylight.

Jack needed to replenish the supply of firewood since he'd used all of it to make the signal. Trying to step as quietly as he could, he moved farther away than before to where the broken branches and fallen trees hadn't yet been gathered, using his wimpy little flashlight to pick his way. He was no longer afraid of shadows in the trees. If he heard movement, he'd know what it was—the female wolf. Silver's mate. Standing guard.

He was no longer afraid of being shot, either, because if anyone out there wanted to shoot him, they'd have done it a lot sooner than this, rather than waiting around in the cold. And he was no longer worried about being lost. The search plane proved that help would soon be coming.

In fact, Jack was feeling pretty good. Firewood lay plentifully on the ground, most of it dry enough to burn. This area had escaped the terrible lightning fires of 1988, when half the park, it seemed, went up in flames. Jack carried armload after armload of wood back to the improvised fireplace. Each time he added fuel, he moved the fire a little closer to the wolf, even though he wasn't sure whether the animal was still breathing. Then, in the golden haze of the fire, Jack saw Silver shudder.

"Hey, boy," he whispered softly. Squatting low, he reached out his hand toward Silver's muzzle. "You OK?"

For the briefest second, Silver's eyes opened. A small sigh of relief escaped Jack's lips.

Even though he knew he shouldn't touch anything that was wild, Jack let his fingers skim the fringe of

Silver's thick coat. What a beautiful animal, Jack thought. In his mind he pictured Silver standing, wind ruffling his coat, on a jut of granite. He felt a surge of, what was it? Awe, yes, awe was what he felt. Up to that second, the wolf had been Troy's. Now, Jack thought, this wolf belongs to all of us. And to none of us.

"Come on, Silver, you're gonna make it," he murmured. "Okay, boy? You've got to live."

Silver's eyes drifted shut; he breathed shallowly, like a dog panting in the hot sun.

Letting his hand rest on Silver's head, Jack raised his eyes toward the sky. At their tops, the tall pines seemed to lean together, like people sharing secrets. In the clear circle at the center of the treetops hung a full, white moon. His breath caught at the beauty of it, at the pleasure of being the only one awake to see it all, and at the privilege of being alone with Silver. Let Troy go on thinking it was just the two of them, Silver and Troy. That would be OK, Jack decided.

After returning to where the others lay sleeping, Jack stacked the fire into a nice, safe, steady burn, then curled himself near it. Almost immediately, he slept again.

Not till the thin edge of the morning sun cleared the mountaintop did the fire's last embers turn to gray ash. Jack awoke feeling chilly, but not chilled to the bone. Troy's face, though, looked pale from cold, and he shivered hard. Then his eyelids flickered open.

"I'll start up the fire again," Jack whispered.

"Is he alive? Silver? I didn't mean to fall asleep." As though it hurt to straighten himself, Troy unwound and crawled onto his knees. He put his cheek right next to the wolf's nose. With wide eyes, he told Jack, "Hey! He's still breathing."

"That's great, Troy," Jack told him.

Instead of being wound up in a tight ball like Troy, Ashley slept curved in a question mark, her face resting against her pressed-together hands. The goose-down parka, good for temperatures as low as -20, had kept her warm enough that her cheeks were pink, not pinched like Troy's.

Jack reached for Troy's torn sneakers, which had sat close to the fire all night long. "They're dry now," he said. "You better put them on." The socks he'd given Troy were made of heavy ragg wool, but with no shoes on, Troy's feet must be like ice cubes, even though he'd huddled close to the fire most of the night. "How do your toes feel?" Jack asked. He hoped they weren't frostbitten.

"Fine. No—actually, my toes are real cold. But they shouldn't break off or anything," he answered with a grin, making it the first time Jack had ever been on the receiving end of a smile from Troy.

As Troy reached for the shoes, one dropped, sending up a puff of wood ash that separated into feathery white flakes before settling back down. Ashley stirred. "Hi, guys," she murmured. "Is Mom here yet?"

"Not yet," Jack answered. Ashley looked so trusting,

as though their mother might appear right that moment out of the trees, carrying a box of Cheerios and three bowls. Or, knowing their mother, with a box of granola and lots of plain yogurt.

Sitting up and stretching her arms, Ashley asked, "How's Silver?"

"Still alive."

"Mom'll fix him up when she gets here."

"I know it."

They didn't have long to wait. By the time Jack had rebuilt a small fire and the entire circle of sun had risen to balance on an eastern peak, they heard the first yells in the distance. "Jack! Ashley! Can you hear us?"

"YEAH!" It was one of those embarrassing times when Jack's deepening voice broke. His squeak sounded like a rooster hit by a barn door.

Troy's voice was all-the-way deep. "Let me," he told them. "WE'RE OVER HERE!"

First Olivia and Steven and Mike yelled. Then Jack and Ashley and Troy gave out answering yells. They kept it up while they ran, closing the gap between them as the yells guided them toward one another, with Troy far in the lead. Olivia and Steven had slid off their horses, and ran forward with their arms outstretched.

"Oh Mommy, I missed you!" Ashley cried as Olivia caught her in a tight hug. "What took you so long?"

That Ashley! Jack thought. No matter how brave she'd acted, she was only a ten-year-old kid who'd very badly wanted her mother. Jack felt his own eyes tear up when he got hugs from both parents. Relief rose in him, all the way up to his throat, because now he could let go and have the grown-ups take over.

Troy hung back awkwardly, watching, shifting from foot to foot in a nervous dance. He waited as long as he could before he burst out, "What about my mom?"

Steven gave Troy a quick hug and said, "No news yet. Maybe we'll hear something when we get back this time."

"At least we found you," Olivia murmured in a choked voice. "I told them it had to be your fire that Dad saw. I said if the kids are out there, Jack will build a signal fire."

"You saw it, Dad?" Jack asked. "You were there in the airplane?"

"Yep," Steven answered. "I made them take me. We flew all over this area. We didn't even spot the fire till three in the morning."

"I know," Olivia told them, "We never even got back from our investigation till nearly ten last night— that's when we reached park headquarters. Park rangers were waiting for us, and when I saw their faces, my heart jumped right into my throat. I've never been so panicked in my life," Olivia said, hugging both her children at the same time. "I prayed and prayed—"

"I wanted to start searching right away on foot,"

Steven said, "but Mike decided we'd do better in the airplane—"

"Were you cold? You must have been starved—"

Everyone was talking all at once, including Mike. "Poor Nicole," he put in, "you know—the ranger who was supposed to meet you? An asphalt truck overturned where they were fixing the road, and she couldn't get past. When she finally made it to the parking lot, you kids were gone. First she was baffled, then later, after she'd searched all over the place and couldn't find you anywhere, she just about freaked."

"Why did you leave the parking lot? You know you weren't supposed to—" Steven began, but Olivia squeezed his arm to silence him.

Slowly, everyone turned to look at Troy.

In a quiet voice, Olivia asked, "Were you trying to run away, Troy?"

Troy's gruff manner came back on him so fast it was as if he'd stepped into a darkened room. "No—is that what you thought?" he demanded. "Is that what you think?"

"But why did you—"

Just then, Mike grabbed his horse's bridle as the mare whinnied and stepped sideways, almost pushing him against a tree. "What is the matter with these horses?" he wondered. "They're all acting like they're scared of something." The other two horses snorted and shook their heads. As one of them backed up, metal poles sticking out from its saddle pack banged against a tree trunk, nicking the bark.

"Watch out!" Mike shouted. "I don't want that stretcher to get bent. Whoa, girl. Take it easy. What is with you?"

Jack knew why the horses were nervous. They smelled wolf. Tugging his mother's hand, he said, "Come on, Mom and Dad. We have something to show you. Mike, you better tie the horses and leave them here."

The sun was bright enough by then that they could catch glimpses of the black wolf, still pacing, but hovering farther away in the shelter of the trees. Now that there were six people coming toward her fallen mate, six humans who talked loudly and made noise as they tramped through the brush, the frightened female abandoned her watch. She turned tail to slink away.

"Oh, no," Olivia said as soon as she reached the wounded wolf. She dropped to her knees beside it. Cautiously, she touched the bloody rib cage. "What happened? Do you know?"

"He got shot," Troy said stiffly.

Nodding, Jack added, "Yeah, we saw him get hit. It happened right after you left."

"Wait a minute, are you saying someone shot a gun in Yellowstone?" Mike barked. "Shooting any kind of firearm is illegal here. Hitting a wolf, an endangered species—well, that's big-time bad! Did you see who did it?"

"No, he was too far away," Ashley told him. "But Troy followed the wolf because he wanted to save its life. And we followed Troy. That's why we weren't waiting for the ranger." Ashley didn't mention how hard they'd tried to keep Troy with them, and all the arguing that had gone on before and after the wolf got shot.

"Oh, Troy," Olivia murmured, "I'm sorry for what I said."

"Forget it," Troy muttered. "Just fix Silver."

Gently parting the animal's fur with her fingers, Olivia examined the wound. "Ashley, you run back to the horses real quick and get my pack. Jack and Troy, you guys better bring the stretcher that's strapped to Mike's saddlebags."

"We thought maybe one of you might be hurt and we'd have to carry you out," Mike explained. "Good thing we brought the stretcher. He'll need it." He gestured toward the wolf.

Steve said, "You kids must be starved. I'll bring some granola bars, too."

Jack almost laughed out loud when he heard that. Granola!

Just what he'd expected.

"And juice," Steve added. "We brought some juice, too."

That sounded better. Jack realized thirst was bothering him more than hunger. The night before, whenever they got thirsty, they'd eaten snow. Although not a lot of snow had fallen before it stopped altogether, they had managed to scoop some where wind had blown small mounds of it against the trees. But after a night spent breathing wood smoke, Jack's throat felt dry and scratchy.

When all of them returned with the supplies, Olivia, still bent over the wolf, murmured, "You kids did a great job. The coldness made the wolf's bleeding nearly stop, yet the fire kept him from freezing. It couldn't have worked any better if I'd had him in the clinic." From her pack she took a syringe, filled it, spurted out a little of the liquid, and injected the needle into the wolf's haunch.

"Cortisone," she explained. "To reduce swelling. There's been a lot of bleeding here." She pointed. "See, it's a grazing wound in the ribs along the chest wall. Good thing it didn't puncture the lung. Ribs will heal, but a penetrating lung wound would have killed him."

"Look at those teeth," Steven exclaimed, pointing to the wolf's partly open mouth. "They're not worn down at all. You can tell he's a young wolf, probably just starting to establish his own pack."

"And strong," Mike said. "That's how he could survive this. He's in beautiful condition."

"Dad, Troy noticed something weird," Jack said. "There's a bullet fragment in the radio collar. Check the battery pack."

Steven leaned over, but Mike got down on all fours to get a closer look. "So he was shot head-on. Looks like an exploding bullet hit the battery pack from the front," Mike said. "Then how did he get wounded in the ribs?"

"Obviously there had to be two shots, one from the front and one from the back. See?" With her finger, Olivia traced the bloody path the bullet had taken, back to front, along the rib cage.

"No, Mom, there was only one shot," Ashley insisted. "Ask Jack. Ask Troy."

Frowning, Mike took off his cap and rubbed his forehead. "Steve, you better take a lot of close-up photographs of the collar and the wound on his side. There's something screwy here."

While Steven photographed the unconscious animal from several angles, Olivia pulled another syringe from her pack. She frowned, shook her head a little, and announced, "I have to tell you, this one scares me. It's a tough call."

"What, Mom?" Jack and Ashley both asked.

"Whether or not I should give him a tranquilizer. If I don't, he might wake up when we move him onto the stretcher, and if he panics he could savage himself and hurt us, too. If I do tranquilize him—and he's already so weak—it might—"

She didn't finish, but Jack knew what she meant. It might kill him.

"You make the call, Olivia," Mike told her. When he saw how worried she looked, he added, "We could tie a bandanna around his muzzle so if he does wake up, he can't bite."

"Yeah, we ought to do that too," Olivia said, "but that part bothers me least. If he wakes up and goes ballistic, he'll start to bleed again." She took a deep breath. "I better do it." After she administered the tranquilizer, she rubbed the wolf's side, then leaned back on her heels.

Mike waited a minute or so before he asked, "Is he out now?"

"He's been pretty much unconscious all along," Olivia answered. "Now he's deeply unconscious. He won't feel a thing when we move him."

"Then I'm gonna pop that radio collar off him. I want to take a better look at it." Mike clicked out the blade of a big hunting knife and used it to unscrew two fasteners that held together the overlapping ends of the collar. When he tugged it, the collar snapped open. He must have done that before, Jack thought, because it looked like he knew what he was doing.

The edges of the rectangular battery pack stuck out in uneven shards. "That had to be one powerful bullet," Mike said. "It's the kind that bursts into fragments on impact." He reached out as though to pull something off the rough edge, then abruptly jerked back his hand.

Troy had been watching the whole procedure closely, as though daring Mike to handle Silver with anything less than the utmost care. "What's wrong?" he asked.

"There's something stuck on his collar. Right here, where the edge is shredded. It's hair."

"So?" Troy asked.

"It's not wolf hair."

All of them crowded around to see, but Mike made them move back. "Get me one of those big plastic bags, Olivia," he said. "The kind you can seal. We need to examine this and see what kind of animal it came from."

"Probably a deer," Steven suggested. "Or maybe a moose calf—whatever the wolf had for lunch."

"I don't think so. Wrong color hair. We'll check it out when we get back." Mike dropped the whole collar into the bag, then sealed it shut.

"OK, time to move him," Olivia decided. She stood up, brushing dirt and pine needles from her jeans. "We need four strong people to carry the stretcher—we'll be going over some rough terrain so it's got to stay as steady as possible."

"I want the stretcher," Troy declared.

"Good—Mike and Steve and Troy and I," Olivia said. "Ashley and Jack, you bring the horses. But before we start—did all you kids get something to eat?"

"I don't want anything." Troy hovered over the wolf until Olivia made him move away. The muscle relaxant and tranquilizer had both started to take effect: the wolf was a floppy, dead weight as they carefully lifted him onto the stretcher. His tongue hung out, long and pink.

When the campfire had been thoroughly extinguished, Jack and Ashley ran down to get the horses. Jack tied the reins of one horse to the saddle horn of another so he could lead two at the same time. Ashley followed with the third.

It was slow going with the wolf, and Jack and Ashley often found themselves far ahead of the others, which was just as well, because the horses were still skittery from the wolf scent. While they waited for the stretcher-bearers to catch up, Jack watched Troy, surprised how sure-footed he was for a city kid, even with those worn-out sneakers. Since the whole trek was downhill and bumpy, maneuvering the stretcher to keep it level was tricky, but Troy managed.

Every so often they stopped so that Olivia could listen to the wolf's heartbeat with a stethoscope, to make sure he was breathing. Each time, from her expression, Jack knew it was OK. So far the wolf was still alive.

When they reached the flat, grassy meadow next to the creek, a helicopter waited, its rotors turning slowly. Not till then did Jack realize how tired he was. Soon they'd be going home, and he could sleep in his own bed. Would home seem the same as it always had? He didn't think so. Not after all that had happened in the past 24 hours.

Then his mother surprised him by saying, "This wolf shooting has complicated things. I'm afraid you kids will have to miss a school day tomorrow. We're going to stay here a little longer to sort things out."

CHAPTER EIGHT

It was past nine in the morning when they reached the tourist cabins at Mammoth Hot Springs. Their gear had already been stowed into two adjoining rooms with a connecting door between.

"Guys in one room; girls in the other," Steven announced, pointing Jack and Troy toward the narrow beds. Jack didn't need much persuasion; he zoned out like a broken circuit the minute his head hit the pillow.

Much later, Troy's prowling awakened him. Groggy, Jack mumbled, "What time is it?"

"Goin' on four," Troy answered. "Your mom's in there waiting for your sister to wake up. Your mom promised I could go see Silver."

"Where's my dad?" Jack asked.

"I dunno. He left with Mike. They kept asking me a lot of questions about the gunshot—saying there had to be two shots. I told them they were wrong."

Still pacing, Troy made a quick turn and knocked over a chair. When it hit the bare wooden floor with a clatter, Olivia cried out from the next room, "What was that?" In a sleepy voice, Ashley echoed, "Yeah. What happened?"

"A chair fell over," Troy called out. From the slight grin that curled Troy's lips, Jack realized it had been no accident. "Did I wake Ashley? Hey, I'm sorry! So can we go see Silver now?"

Jack sat up on the side of the bed and began to pull on his boots. "I'll be ready right away," he said.

Looking a bit apologetic, Olivia came into the room. "Sorry, not this time," she told Jack. "Too many visitors at once would spook the wolf. Even though he's conscious now, he's still pretty much traumatized." Smoothing Jack's tousled hair, she added softly, "I already promised Troy he could be the first one to visit. You and Ashley will get your turns; you'll just have to wait."

Jack might have been more disappointed if his father hadn't arrived just at that moment, shoving open the cabin door. He'd been waiting for a chance to tell his dad about the wolf pictures.

"You're up, Jack. Good!" Steven said. "Mike wants to ask you something."

"About the rifle shot? I'll tell him the same thing Troy did. There was only one shot."

"You sure?"

"Yeah. And Dad, I didn't tell this you before, but I took some pictures of where the guy was standing. The guy with the gun. I mean, I didn't take pictures of him, because I couldn't really see him. He was too far away and I only had my little point-and-shoot camera and anyway he was hiding in the trees. But at least it will show where he was."

"Mmmmm." Steven frowned. "I'll let Mike know."

"But Dad," Jack continued, "this is even more important. I think I got some really great pictures of the wolf. When are we going home so you can develop the film for me?"

Steven was still thinking hard. "We'll be here at least till early tomorrow morning," he said. "But I think there's a working photo lab in the park administration building. Maybe we ought to develop your film right here, right now."

"Why, Dad? I don't want anything to mess up those wolf negatives!"

"Because there might be a chance—just a small chance—that we could see something on the pictures of the guy with the gun. I know it's a long shot—" Steven laughed. "Yeah, it really was a long shot for your camera, wasn't it—300 or 400 hundred yards? Or maybe more than that. And he was hiding in shadow. But sometimes— you never know—pictures can be computer-enhanced to bring out details you wouldn't otherwise see. Where's the film?"

Jack handed over his camera, then crossed the room to stick his head under the cold-water faucet at the small sink. The sink was the only "facility" in the cabin. For showers and other plumbing, they needed to hike across the parking lot to the bathhouse. Jack felt pretty grimy and he smelled like a campfire, but since Steven seemed to be in a hurry, he just doused his face with cold water. That woke him up fast.

He was rubbing his head with a towel when Olivia came back into the room. "Before you guys go," she said, "we need to coordinate our plans. Troy's going with me. Jack's going with you, Steve. What about Ashley?"

"I guess she better come along with Jack and me," Steven answered.

"OK. Let's all try to meet at the hotel lobby by 5:30. These kids need a good meal. Troy, come on. We can leave now." As Troy followed Olivia through the door to the outside, he asked her, "Can we call the police about my mother before we go see Silver?"

Steven shook his head slightly, a look Olivia caught. "Why don't we wait till a little later for that, Troy?" she suggested. "We want to get to the wolf pen before the sun's too low."

After they'd gone, Steven asked, "Ready, kids?"

"Ready." Their parkas would be too warm now, so both of them pulled on the thick sweatshirts Olivia had packed for them. While they walked along the paved road toward the administration building, Steven remarked, "Poor Troy. He keeps asking, and I hate to have to keep telling him—we still don't know what happened to his mother. The longer we don't hear anything, the more likely it is that she just took off and abandoned him."

"No way, Dad," Ashley said. "Last night Troy told us all about his mom. She'd never just leave him."

Steven didn't answer, but he looked down at Ashley in that grown-up way both kids hated, as though innocent children couldn't possibly understand the ways of the real world. Jack was about to add, "She's right, Dad," but his father's expression dampened the words before they came out. Sometimes it was adults who just didn't understand. Or didn't trust enough.

As they neared the building they saw Mike hurriedly crossing the road toward them.

"Hey, Mike. What's the rush?" Steven asked him.

"Tryin' to get away from those guys." Mike tossed his head toward a rusty pickup truck, with huge tires, peeling out of the parking lot. Inside the cab, three big men were crammed together.

"Who are they?"

"A posse of angry ranchers."

"What'd they want from you?" Steven asked.

"I didn't wait to find out. Soon as I opened the door and heard them yellin' inside about wolves endangering their livestock, I just turned around and scooted right back out." Mike grinned guiltily over his narrow escape. "I did hear one thing, though, before I closed the door. They were saying George Campbell's dog, the one that got killed by the wolves, was worth a thousand dollars."

"A thousand? We heard him say 500 on the radio," Jack mentioned.

"Shoot! I know for a fact," Mike told them, "Campbell got the dog from an old rancher who lives out past Gardiner, and that rancher never charged more than 20 bucks for a weaned pup. I have an idea the price goes up every time George Campbell tells his story." Mike chuckled, then asked, "Where are you guys off to now?"

Steven held out his hand to show Mike the roll of film and answered, "Jack and I need to develop this. He took a few pictures that might show something useful, if we're lucky. But probably not."

"How 'bout if I borrow Ashley for a while?" Mike suggested. "I'd like to check out what each of the three kids remembers about the shooting, one at a time. I can take her to the ice-cream shop—"

"Yes!" Ashley cried. "I've got a great memory! I'll tell you everything that happened."

Steven rolled his eyes. "Ashley'll confess to anything if you buy her a chocolate sundae. We're meeting at the Lodge at 5:30, Mike."

"Sounds good. See you then."

The darkroom was located in the basement—darkrooms were almost always in basements, because less outside light reached them that way. After Steven checked all the equipment and jugs of chemical solutions, he turned out the lights to begin processing the film.

Jack remembered the first time his father had taken him into their darkroom at home. He'd been not quite eight years old, and excited to be initiated into the mysteries of his father's work. The total blackness hadn't frightened him because he could sense his father's nearness, and all the while, Steven kept talking, explaining everything he did.

At that time Jack had been reading a book about the first Indians who'd lived near the Teton Mountains, deep inside caves lit only by small, smoky fires. If the fires went out, the caves became so black that nothing real could be seen, but after a while, the eyes of the imagination played tricks, and real-looking images would appear before them in the darkness. They thought it was magic. Then Indian fathers would tell their sons about hunting with spears and arrows, and teach them to beg forgiveness of the animals they killed for food.

Two thousand years later, when Jack first stood in the total blackness of his father's darkroom, and Steven explained to him how to develop film, he'd thought of those early Indians in their dark caves. Because images began to appear to Jack then, growing clearer and clearer in the developer trays. They were the animals

Steven had captured on film with his camera. Watching them come forth from blank paper, shaping themselves into bears and cougars and bison right in front of his eyes—it had seemed like magic to Jack, too.

Now he waited, hoping that his own pictures would turn out perfect. In his mind's eye, in this darkness, he remembered how the wolf had stared at him with those yellow eyes, alert and unafraid. He wanted to show his mother just how majestic the wolf had been before the bullet slammed against his body. As his father lifted the strip of color negatives from the stabilizer solution, Jack crossed his fingers. Were they any good?

He lost all track of time. After the negatives dried, his father let Jack put them into the enlarger. There were ten prints. The four of the mule deer when the wolves had chased it across the creek were too out of focus to be any good. There were three of the wolf, and three others of where the gunman had stood. The rest of the negatives, blank because they were unexposed, Jack threw away.

They loaded paper into the tube and began to process the prints. When the lights came on and the prints emerged from the processor, Jack let out the breath he'd been holding. The wolf pictures were going to be beautiful! He waited for his father to exclaim over them, but Steven just stood there, acting puzzled.

"I don't get this," Steven said.

"Dad!" It was a cry of disappointment. "What about

my wolf shots? Are any of them any good?"

"What! Oh—Jack—they're so good I'll need a half hour just to tell you how great they are. It's these other pictures I can't figure out."

"I know the deer pictures are out of focus— it was moving too fast."

"No—these." Steven held up the strip of negatives to examine them. "First I thought maybe it was a flaw in the film, but the negatives are fine. Look at that—" He pointed. "In the negs it's a little green dot; in the prints it's a bright red dot. It's on all three pictures of where you said the gunman was standing."

Lifting the wet prints carefully, one by one, touching them only on the corners, Jack saw what his father meant. Each of the three prints showed foothills, a clump of pine trees—and a red dot in the middle of the trees. The dots were tiny, like pinpoints of red light, although one of them seemed to have a small halo around it.

"Maybe it's sun reflecting off something," Jack suggested, but Steven answered, "No, sunlight reflects white, not red. Oh well, you ought to be really happy with your wolf pictures, son. As soon as we get home, I'm going to enlarge them and frame them for your room. But we gotta go now to meet your mom and Troy and Mike and Ashley, so we'll let these prints dry and pick them up later.

"Take the negatives!" Jack insisted. Prints weren't too

important—he could always make extra prints, as many as he wanted. Negatives, though, were irreplaceable.

Everyone met in the hotel lobby and then hurried across the street to the restaurant, because by that time the kids were really starved. At least Jack was; Troy looked gloomy and Ashley had already eaten a chocolate sundae, so maybe she wasn't too hungry.

After they ordered, Mike said, "Take a look out the windows, guys. We have visitors."

A herd of elk had arrived at the restaurant for dinner, too, but they were dining on the front lawn, literally. A big bull elk, with an impressive rack of antlers, lay comfortably on his belly, chewing his cud and wiggling his ears to drive away flies. His harem of three elk cows stood nearby, heads down, munching the lawn. Two middle-size calves faced away from them, providing a super view of their pale rumps to the watchers at the restaurant window.

Olivia put her arm around Troy's shoulders. "These are the animals I work with, Troy, down at the Elk Refuge in Jackson Hole. Every winter whole herds of them migrate from Yellowstone to get fed at the refuge. And they don't just come from here. They come from all the higher ranges in the Tetons, too. We get 10,000 head of elk coming into the refuge every winter, and for each animal, each day, we put out 10 pounds of hay."

"Hay! That's a lot!" Ashley joked.

Troy didn't answer.

A day ago Jack would have thought he was just being surly; now he realized how much Troy was hurting inside, about his mother.

"If we didn't help feed them, a lot of the elk would starve over the winter," Olivia said.

Across the road an even bigger bull elk, with even grander antlers, shook himself and pawed the ground with his right front hoof. He seemed to be putting on a lusty display for the benefit of the cows. As he bent down to scrape his antlers against the grass, his powerful shoulder muscles bunched up; then he lifted his head and bugled. Even from inside the restaurant, with the doors and windows closed, his bugling sounded impressive.

"I like wolf song better," Ashley admitted.

Their food arrived then, and the six of them sat around the table, eating and talking—all except Troy, who didn't do much of either.

"How were Jack's pictures?" Olivia asked.

"Your son," Steven answered, "is one of the world's great junior photographers. As soon as we're finished here I'll go get the prints of his wolf pictures. But you know," he said, turning to Mike, "there's something that's weird about the other pictures—the ones Jack took of the mountain. Right in the middle of all three prints is a little red dot. I can't figure out what it came from."

Mike shrugged. "Maybe somebody dropped a bandanna on the ground."

"No, it looked more like a light."

"Ashley said she saw a shirt through the binoculars—" Olivia began.

"The shirt wasn't red, Mom. It was blue plaid. Too bad I couldn't see the face of the person wearing it."

"I couldn't guess what the red spot was, then," Mike said. "But I have to tell you, your Ashley makes a great witness. She convinced me you kids heard only one shot. And then she came up with a question that got me thinking."

"What question was that?" Troy asked, talking with his mouth full.

"Ashley wanted to know why we couldn't take the bullet fragment from the radio collar and the bullet from the wolf's wound and see if they matched. In the first place, we don't have the bullet that hit the wolf's side. It was a grazing wound, so the bullet just skimmed off somewhere."

"Good thing it did," Olivia said. "If it had penetrated, Silver would have died."

"Right. Silver is one lucky wolf," Mike continued, "in a lot of ways. Because that first bullet, the one that hit the collar, is what we call a hot bullet—it was made to fragment on impact at close range. Looking at the way it tore up the battery pack, I'd say that bullet came in at an angle, too. When it hit, it blew into fragments, but the battery pack absorbed most of the energy. I'm sure Silver got knocked down from the impact—you know, like when a policeman wearing a bullet-proof vest gets shot at? The bullet doesn't go in, but it slams him to the ground."

"I did notice he had some blood spots around his collar," Olivia said.

"I guess it was from a few tiny bullet fragments striking him through his thick fur."

Mike put down his fork and added, "Anyway, I started to wonder just when that first shot was fired. The one that hit the collar. Was it yesterday, or even before that?"

This time they all stopped eating to pay attention to Mike.

"I realized," he went on, "that this was the same wolf whose signal stopped transmitting a couple of days ago. His radio collar went silent on the day George Campbell's dog was attacked. So I thought, is that just a coincidence? Maybe. Or maybe not. And then—"

"I asked him about the hair," Ashley said. "I said, 'What color was that hair that was stuck on Silver's collar?'"

Olivia frowned. "What are you suggesting, Mike? That it was dog hair? Golden retriever?"

"Could have been. I think it might be smart if we paid a visit to George Campbell and picked up a sample of his dog's hair to see if it matches."

"His dog is dead," Troy said.

"Dogs shed hair. If he stayed in a doghouse, there'd be plenty of hair inside it. Most likely it won't match what was on Silver's collar, and even if it does, I don't know just what that would prove, exactly."

"Well, if it was the dog's hair, that would prove the collar had to be shot before the dog attack, wouldn't it?" Jack exclaimed. "The hair wouldn't stick to the radio collar if it was smooth. Only if it had jagged edges from being blown apart."

Mike shrugged. "It's a mystery. And there's another mystery we didn't tell you kids about. You know how we went searching for the dog's remains yesterday? We rode to the exact place where Campbell reported the attack happened. Well, we didn't find any dog remains."

"We went back and forth along the border between Gallatin National Forest and Yellowstone National Park—" Olivia began.

"Three times," Steven broke in. "We split up and scoured the whole area, a good couple of miles in all directions from the spot Campbell pointed out on the map in Mike's office—"

"That's why we were so late getting back," Olivia continued. "We searched it thoroughly, but we couldn't find a thing. I guess Mr. Campbell was mixed up about where it actually happened. I mean, there's no visible boundary marker that a person would notice, especially with a pack of wolves chasing him."

"Anyway, I know where Campbell lives," Mike said. "Anyone want to come with me? We can all drive there in the park van."

Jack, Troy, Mike, and Steven all shoved back their chairs at the same time and stood up. Olivia got up, too, and answered, "Definitely. There are a lot of questions I'd like to ask Mr. Campbell. Like, how old was his dog, and was it in good health? Wolves often attack an animal when they sense it's weak—if it's sick or limping or something."

"Yeah, and I'd like to ask him if he saw any of those demonstrators in the woods the day his dog was attacked," Mike added. "If it turned out to be the same day the wolf's collar got hit, Campbell might be able to give us a lead on who did the shooting. A militia member, or an angry rancher, or anyone he noticed carrying a rifle—"

"Dad, please, let's pick up my prints before we go," Jack begged.

"Good idea," Troy said. "I want to see the pictures of my wolf."

CHAPTER NINE

Go on, keep them," Jack told Troy. "I can make a ton more prints if I want to."

"Thanks!" Troy clutched the wolf pictures as if it were Christmas and he'd just been given the keys to Wal-Mart. He stared at them for five full minutes as the van wound along the road toward the park's north gate. Then, with much less interest, Troy examined the other three pictures.

"Weird!" he said. "Red dots in the middle of each picture. Must be something wrong with your camera."

"No way," Jack argued. "If it was the camera, there'd be red dots in the wolf pictures, too. And they are fine." More than fine, he added in his own mind. They're the best I've ever taken.

Troy shrugged and handed the prints back to Jack, except for the wolf pictures, which he continued to grip tightly in his hand.

"Let me see," Ashley said. "The red dot ones." She studied them for a long while before shoving them into the pocket of her sweatshirt. By then, her lips and eyes had both started to pucker. "How much farther?" she asked, looking more and more uncomfortable. No wonder, Jack thought, since she'd had a full dinner on top of a chocolate sundae, and the road kept twisting and turning enough to make anyone a little carsick. Jack was glad Ashley had picked the seat right next to a back window. If she really felt bad, she wouldn't have to crawl over him to reach fresh air.

"About ten more miles," Mike answered. "The last part will be on an unpaved road." He glanced at the rear-view mirror to check Ashley—from the sound of her voice, he must have been able to tell she was queasy. Mike probably had kids of his own, Jack thought, who got carsick on roads like these. "George Campbell owns a run-down little ranch a few miles from here. He stays on the ranch but he doesn't raise cattle anymore. I don't know how he makes a living."

"So he's not one of the mean, nasty ranchers who hate wolves," Ashley said.

"Hey, wait a minute!" Mike glanced quickly at the three kids in the back seat. "Ranchers aren't mean and nasty—at least the vast majority of ranchers aren't. You need to realize they make their living raising cattle and sheep. When a wolf takes down one of their livestock, it's a serious loss to them."

"Oh," Ashley said meekly.

"Just figure," Mike went on, "if the rancher has a cow that could be auctioned off for $500, but a wolf kills it first. Maybe, then, the rancher won't be able to afford new tires for his pickup that winter, or college books for his daughter at Montana State."

"I'm sorry," Ashley began, her lips held stiffly, either because she was getting ready to cry or maybe throw up.

Jack hoped she wouldn't do either.

"Naturally, when there's any controversy, I most often take the side of the wolves," Mike explained, grinning. "Not surprising, since I'm a wolf biologist. I've spent the past few years of my life trying to make this reintroduction program work. But don't go thinking ranchers and their families are the bad guys. They're not. They're just regular people trying to—"

The last words broke off as Ashley rapidly lowered the window, stuck out her head, and took some deep breaths.

"You OK?" Jack asked.

Olivia glanced back nervously, but Ashley gasped, "I'm fine." She slumped back into the seat.

After they bumped four or five more miles down an unpaved road, with Ashley's face pressed against the partly opened windowpane, Mike stopped the van. "We're here," he announced.

They were parked in shadow, at least a hundred

yards from the dilapidated ranch house.

No one made a move to get out. Through the gray dusk, they all watched a dimly lit window behind the front porch. The curtains moved, but no one came to the door, and the evening stayed silent, with not even a bark from a dog. But then, George Campbell's dog could no longer bark.

"You know," Mike finally said, "I think I'll take a little walk around the place. I'd like to check...." He didn't finish. "You guys want to wait in the van? Or maybe, since Ashley's feeling kind of green around the gills, you might want to wait outside in the fresh air."

"Good idea," Steven said. "OK, everybody out."

As Mike took off into the darkness, the Landons stood together at the bottom of the driveway, if you could call it that. It was nothing more than a twin-rutted dirt track that led up to the front door.

George Campbell's small house was made of wood that had dried to the color of chicken bones. Right away Jack noticed how beaten down the house looked. Suddenly Troy exclaimed, "Hey, everybody, look over there!"

In one corner of the yard stood a doghouse as weathered as the Campbell home. A rusty metal chain snaked from inside it to wind around an empty water dish. Propped against the side of the doghouse was a large cardboard tombstone made from what Jack guessed was a refrigerator box. A can of black spray paint lay tipped over on the ground nearby, next to a paint-stained rag. The sign read:

Rex

MURDERED BY WOLVES
Your dog could be next.
Or YOU!

"Oh, please," Olivia groaned, color rising to her face. Steven reached out and squeezed her elbow lightly. "Stay cool, lady. Blow it off. It's just a publicity stunt."

"Now we know there's a doghouse," Jack said. "So we can collect some of Rex's hair."

Walking close together, they approached the crudely lettered monument to Rex. "I just gotta get some pictures of that," Steven said. "Jack, stand over on that side and hold the strobe light so we don't get too much shadow."

As Jack took his position where his father told him to, Steven fired off about ten shots from different angles.

When he finished, Olivia got down on her knees. "Looks like there's plenty of hair inside. We'll have to ask Mr. Campbell if he'll allow us to take a sample."

None of them noticed the man who'd stepped out onto the front porch. "No need to stand in the cold. Come on in," he yelled. When they whirled around to stare, they saw him rotating his hands like a traffic cop, urging them to move forward. "Come on, come on."

"That has to be George Campbell," Olivia said softly. "He certainly seems anxious to get us in his house."

"I guess it's ok," Steven answered. "Mike will figure out we've gone inside."

As they moved up the dirt driveway Steven added, "Jack, hang on to my camera—carefully!—while I fit this strobe back into the camera case. And when we get in the house, I don't want you kids to say a single word except 'hello.' You got that? Just keep quiet and stay still. You can look around as much as you want to, but don't move around."

The stairs up to the porch sagged forward; as Jack walked up them he felt slightly off-balance. His parents paused on the top step while Troy, Ashley, and Jack jostled for position behind them.

"Howdy!" George Campbell was a big man, tall and heavyset, and he had a big voice. "Come in, come in, come in," he almost shouted. Then, rubbing his hand over his stubbly chin, he said, "Guess you saw my sign over there. I noticed you out here takin' pictures."

"We did," Olivia answered calmly. "We're all very sorry about your dog."

"Demon wolves," he grunted, as he led them inside. "They killed my dog and could have killed me. I'm tryin' to rally some right-thinking citizens to get together and demand that every last one of those critters gets exterminated."

Blinking hard, Olivia followed Mr. Campbell. The

rest of them filed in behind her, and the screen door banged shut.

The inside of the house was as dark and cramped as Jack imagined it would be. To the left stood a wood-burning stove. On all four walls hung stuffed heads of deer and elk. One wall held a bison head, and next to it the mounted head of a young grizzly bear. Where had he gotten that, Jack wondered. Glass eyes seemed to follow them as Mr. Campbell motioned Olivia and Steven to sit on a sofa with a faded knit afghan thrown over the top.

Ashley perched on the end of the sofa while Steven and Olivia sank low in the sagging middle. Jack and Troy hung back against the wall.

"You kids want to sit?" Campbell asked, pointing to the floor.

Nudging Jack with his elbow, Troy shook his head quickly.

"No thanks," Jack told him. "We've been sitting a long time. We'll just stand over here."

"Suit yourself," the man said, eyeing the camera in Jack's hand and the camera case Steven set on the floor.

The boys took positions on either side of a tall cabinet, the only new, expensive-looking piece of furniture in the room. Behind the glass front stood four high-powered hunting rifles. One, with a long black barrel, looked like it could blow a hole in brick. Troy stared at the cabinet, then glanced toward George

Campbell. From the tense way Troy pressed backward against the wall, with his palms flat against the rough wood paneling, Jack could tell that something about the gun case had excited him. But what?

Clearing her throat, Olivia leaned forward. She had a small tape recorder in her hand. "Do you mind if I tape our interview, Mr. Campbell? I find it very helpful."

"Go right ahead," George agreed. "I already told my story a hundred times, but I don't mind saying it again and again until somebody listens and does something about it. I've collected over $600 from people like me who hate those wolves. I'm planning on telling the whole world about—"

"Six hundred dollars?" Olivia asked.

"That's just from people who heard me on talk radio. The newspapers will be even better."

What an old buzzard, Jack thought. His mother had pressed a button, and was holding the recorder in Campbell's direction. "OK, Mr. Campbell. Would you like to talk about exactly what happened that day, step by step, starting with what you were doing in Yellowstone?"

"Hiking. I'm a—you know—a nature lover."

Yeah, right, Jack thought. He didn't listen to any more, but let his eyes slide over onto Troy, who was still staring intently at the gun case.

"....no call for the government to tramp all over the rights of law-abiding citizens—"

"Mr. Campbell," Olivia broke in. "Let's get back to your dog and the wolves."

"Sure. Right. I get carried away. So...which newspaper are you from?"

Everyone froze. So that's why George Campbell was being so friendly! He'd noticed the camera, had seen them taking pictures of the doghouse, and mistakenly thought they worked for a newspaper! They all waited, staying perfectly quiet—even Ashley—to see what Olivia would do.

"We...uh...work in Jackson Hole," she answered.

So she was going to fake it! Jack bit his lip to keep from grinning.

"Good!" George Campbell exclaimed. "The further this story reaches, the better. At midnight tonight I'm gonna be on talk radio in Denver." Since he was oblivious to anyone but himself, Campbell hadn't noticed the nervously exchanged glances, the bated breaths, and he didn't notice it now when they all started breathing again.

Troy was moving his lips, trying to say something silently to Jack, but Jack couldn't make it out. Troy shook his head impatiently and mouthed the words again. Jack still didn't understand.

Moving slowly around to the other side of the cabinet, Jack got close to Troy and flattened himself against the wall the way Troy was doing. "What?" he whispered.

"Look at that rifle barrel," Troy breathed.

Jack's voice was so low he could barely hear himself. "Which one? I don't know guns."

"Yeah? I do. That 308 in there'll blast a hole the size of a dinner plate. But check out this rifle!" With his finger, Troy traced a path along the glass to point at a silver tube, only a couple inches long, that had been mounted beneath the barrel of one of the rifles.

"Hey—what is this? What are you kids doin' over there?" Campbell's eyebrows knit together in a dark line as he glared at Jack and Troy. "Get them away from my guns," he told Steven. "Those things are valuable, and I don't want the kids fooling with them. I'll get sued if they blow their heads off."

"Jack, Troy, don't touch anything," Steven ordered them.

"We just want to look," Troy said. "They're...cool."

"You bet they are." George Campbell nodded. "Nothin's better than a powerful gun. You go on and look, but mind you don't do more than that."

Satisfied, George Campbell turned around with his back to the boys and started right in again. Olivia didn't have to ask him any questions at all, because Campbell needed no encouragement. He was a talker. Give him an audience, and his mouth took over.

But Troy was growing agitated. Moving his head a little toward Campbell, he whispered, "Check the shirt."

It was a gray sweatshirt with a team logo. "Oakland Raiders," Jack said.

"No! The one he's got on underneath!"

Although the gray sweatshirt reached all the way up to Campbell's neck and down to his wrists, hanging out from the bottom edge in back was a bit of shirttail, wrinkled and limp. Then Jack saw it. The shirttail was blue plaid.

"Yes!" Jack hissed. "That's the same color the shooter had!"

Troy's jaw clenched and his face reddened. Suddenly, he took two steps forward and yelled, "You—you shot Silver. And you pointed your gun at my friend Jack. You jerk!"

"What?" George Campbell sputtered. "Are you talkin' to me?"

"Yeah. You, man!"

Jack stared at Troy, shocked by the rage burning in his face. Then the words penetrated, and Jack felt a sensation like ice in his chest. Was it true what Troy was saying, that George Campbell had pointed his high-powered rifle at Jack?

"The red dot! The red dot!" Troy was shouting. "It came from the laser sight on that rifle right there. He was pointing it right at Jack when Jack took the pictures."

"Pictures? What pictures?" George Campbell asked loudly.

"We got lots of pictures. We got pictures of the wolf, and of you aiming that laser sight right at Jack," Troy hollered. "Holding a gun on a kid! How's that gonna sound on talk radio?"

The big man reeled backward. "Don't be crazy! I'd never shoot a kid!"

"We got proof. We saw you, and we heard you, and we got it on film. You shooting Silver in your blue plaid shirt." It seemed as if Troy's fury would split his skin.

"My...shirt?" George Campbell's eyes darted around the room before glancing down. He hurriedly shoved his shirttail into his pants.

"It was you," Ashley cried. "I saw you in the binoculars! "You tried to kill Silver."

"Now look, maybe you got pictures of me with a gun, but I swear, shootin' the wolf—that was—uh, accidental. The gun went off when it bumped against a tree," Campbell said, speaking not to Ashley, but to Olivia and Steven as though kids didn't matter; only adults needed explanations. "You say you got a picture of that?"

"Accidental? We got pictures of you pointing the gun at Jack!" Troy yelled. "You could have blown a hole right through him!"

Campbell whipped around to face the boys. "Nah, it wasn't anything like that. See, what I was doin'—" Again he turned toward Steven and Olivia, declaring, "I was just usin' my rifle's spotting scope like a telescope 'cause I heard someone yellin' and I was tryin' to see who it was. A spotting scope—you know—magnifies. The laser sight wasn't even on."

"Sure it was," Jack said hotly. His anger mounted, too, as Campbell tried to worm out of what he'd done. This man, who'd almost killed Silver and could have killed Jack himself, was lying right to their faces. "Your laser sight showed up real clear in the pictures I took yesterday when you shot the wolf."

Bluffing, he held his father's camera high. "See this lens? It can focus a quarter of a mile away. Right, Dad?"

"Yeah. That's right." Steven replied haltingly, as though he wasn't sure what his lines were supposed to be in this scene, but he hoped he was getting them right. "It's a special lens for long-distance nature photography," he said. He didn't add that he'd never dream of letting Jack use that expensive lens by himself, and that the camera Jack had yesterday was nothing more than a little point-and-shoot that couldn't even zoom.

Jack could hardly believe what was happening! First Olivia had bluffed, and now the rest of them were faking it, too, and somehow they'd stumbled onto the unexpected fact that George Campbell had been there, yesterday, pointing a gun when Silver got shot! And the man was admitting it!

"Look folks, it was all accidental! I swear! I'll stand before a judge and so-help-me-God I'll tell him I never meant to shoot that wolf—"

"You're lying! Our pictures prove you meant to kill Silver," Ashley cried, jumping up and waving the prints.

"We got the red dot right here—"

"Don't show him!" Jack yelled, but it was one of those times when Ashley decided to ignore her brother.

"No!" Jack cried. He lunged at her, but it was too late. She'd already handed the prints to Campbell.

"What? These?" As he shuffled the prints—one, two, three—like winning cards in a poker hand, Campbell laughed out loud.

"You call this evidence? You can't see nothin' in those pictures." Striding across the room, he pulled open the door of the wood-burning stove and tossed them inside.

"We still have the negatives," Jack said defiantly.

Campbell left the stove door open. Heat from the flames reflected in his face as he turned on them and roared, "You can't fool me. You're not from the newspaper! This is a government conspiracy. You come in here with fake pictures that say I shot a wolf—well, I say—prove it! In court! Half the hunters in this state own laser sights on their rifles, and you couldn't tell it was me anyways 'cause I was standing way back in the trees and I don't even show in those pictures. I'll deny it all. You got nothing on me!"

Surrounded by his animal heads, seeming to grow larger in the flickering shadows like a villain in a bad movie, George Campbell sneered, "So how you gonna prove anything, huh?"

No one answered, because they all knew the answer,

all except George Campbell. Suddenly he figured it out, too. As he focused on the tape recorder in Olivia's hand, his eyes grew wide. "Hey! Give me that thing!" he bellowed.

He lunged toward Olivia. Before Steven could unwind himself from the sagging sofa, Troy and Jack leaped in front of Campbell, blocking him. "This is my house," Campbell screamed. "You can't come in here and—I'm a law-abiding citizen! I want that tape recorder, or you're not getting out of here."

"Are you threatening us?" Olivia asked him, jumping up.

Steven was on his feet too, swerving in front of her to protect her.

George Campbell weighed more than Troy and Jack put together. For a few seconds the big man strained against them, pushing forward as the boys struggled to hold him back. He was so tall....

"Give—me—that—tape," Campbell grunted.

Jack tried to grip his arm, but Campbell clutched him and yanked Jack back against his armpit, nearly choking him. "Hey—let me go!" Jack's yelling was muffled as Campbell squeezed him tighter.

"Let go of them!" Steven demanded, grappling with Campbell, trying to break his hold on the boys.

"OW! Dang it!" Campbell yelled and swore, because Troy was stomping on his foot. In a sudden move he butted both boys with his shoulders, knocking them loose so that they staggered. At the same time he shoved Steven hard. But before he could push past Steven to reach Olivia, Ashley grabbed the tape recorder from her mother's hand. Quick as lightning, she dashed across the room and yanked open the door.

On the porch she nearly collided with Mike, who was on his way in.

"What's goin' on here?" Mike cried.

"He shot the wolf!"

"We got it on tape."

"Good thing you're here—"

One voice yelled, "They're all lyin'!"

Everyone was shouting at once, but Mike raised his hand and said, "Hold it! I've already got the sheriff's office on the line."

He held Olivia's cellular phone next to his face with his left hand as he pointed to George Campbell with his right. "They were real interested when I told them about that pickup truck full of antlers I saw out back."

"You searched my property!" George Campbell screamed. "You can't do that without a warrant."

"I didn't open anything, didn't touch anything, just happened to notice. The sheriff'll be the one to investigate, and he'll be out here any minute with your warrant. But that truck—my, my! Loaded with deer antlers, elk antlers, moose racks," Mike went on. "That's what you were doing in Yellowstone—gathering horn. Unlawful, buddy, and you know it. And now you topped it off by shooting a wolf?" Mike shook his head and clucked his tongue. "You're in a world of hurt, man."

"You can't prove anything," Campbell sneered.

Mike rocked back on his heels, pushing against Ashley, who'd taken refuge behind him. "Wanna bet?" He grinned. "For starters, we've been marking certain antlers with fluorescent paint for a couple of years now just to catch thieves like you." To Steven, he said, "He must have a few hundred pounds of horn out there. It sells for ten bucks a pound around here, but a whole lot more than that when it gets shipped to Asia. He's going to need every penny to pay a lawyer."

Headlights bumped up and down as a sheriff's cruiser navigated the narrow rutted drive toward the ranch house.

At that point George Campbell must have realized it would be smart to keep his mouth shut. He glowered at everyone, but he didn't speak another word.

CHAPTER TEN

It was ten o'clock at night, but after all the excitement, no one was the least bit sleepy. As the van headed back toward Yellowstone Park, everyone inside tried to talk at the same time.

"What is a laser sight?" Ashley demanded. "I don't even know."

Steven answered her. "It's a targeting device that beams a narrow red light on whatever the hunter's aiming at. The hunter takes aim through his spotting scope, turns on the laser sight, and whatever that red dot lands on—that's exactly where the bullet's going to hit when he squeezes the trigger. It's deadly accurate."

"How'd you know about it, Troy?" Jack asked.

"You can put 'em on handguns, too. Back in my old neighborhood, a lot of guys used them."

"Oh."

No one commented, but Jack wondered if they

were thinking what he was—that it would be tough to live in a neighborhood where people ran around carrying guns. Using guns. Where a small red dot on a shirt front would mark where a bullet was about to rip through someone's chest.

"Still," Olivia told Troy, "it was very smart of you to connect the red lights on the pictures with the laser sight on Campbell's rifle."

"Yeah," Troy agreed. "But Jack's the one who snowed him about the camera lens. That was cool."

"What about me?" Ashley asked. "I bet George Campbell would have tossed Mom's recorder right into the fire!"

Troy nodded. "You did good, too."

"So what's going to happen to Campbell?" Jack wanted to know.

Mike answered, "I'm not sure yet. Carrying a gun and bringing a dog into the park—they're just misdemeanors. Picking up antlers and taking them out of the park to sell—that's a bigger crime. But shooting a wolf, an endangered species—that's a big-time federal offense. We'll build a real tight case against him."

"Want to hear my theory about what really happened?" Olivia asked.

When they all answered yes, she said, "Here's the way I reconstruct it. Campbell was in the park gathering horn, letting his dog run loose. Silver and his mate were nearby, probably minding their own business." Olivia paused. "He said a wolf pack attacked his dog, but I don't believe that."

"Why, Mom?" Jack asked.

"I think Silver and his mate had just recently broken away from their old pack to start a new pack of their own. That's what happens when young, strong, smart wolves mate. After they have pups, it will be the beginning of a new wolf pack in Yellowstone."

"Ooooh! Can we come back and see the pups next year?" Ashley exclaimed.

"If...things work out." Olivia looked back at Ashley as if she'd been about to say more, but decided against it.

Jack was pretty sure he knew what his mother was thinking. If! If Silver survived, and became healthy enough to hunt food for his mate and the pups, there'd be a new pack in Yellowstone. But Silver might never be strong enough again to hunt, even for himself.

"Go on with your theory, Olivia," Steven urged her, nodding.

"Well, I think Campbell's dog saw the two wolves— just those two, not a whole pack—and decided to chase them. The dog, Rex, chased the wolves—not the other way around. Campbell took the first shot that hit Silver's collar. Then Silver and his mate turned on the dog and killed it, and that's when Rex's hair got stuck on the ripped-up part of the collar."

"So why didn't he shoot Silver again, right then?" Troy asked.

Jack guessed the answer to that one. "Too scared. He thought the wolves would turn around and come after him next. He made a run for it."

"Yeah, he ran straight to my office to scream about his dog being killed," Mike said. "Right off, he demanded money for it. Made up that story about Rex being chased across the boundary, and lied some more when he showed me the wrong place on the map. I told Campbell the park's budget wasn't set up to pay for a pet's death. That got him really mad."

Troy took over. "He's not getting money, so the guy wants revenge. The next day he comes gunning for Silver. He's got this laser sight on his rifle, he takes aim, and—pow! Nearly kills Silver."

"Oh man!" Mike slapped the steering wheel. "Are we gonna nail Campbell good! The first time he shot Silver, when the bullet hit the radio collar, well, he can probably weasel out of that one. He'll probably claim self-defense. But coming back a day later to intentionally shoot an endangered-species animal—that's a major criminal violation. It's clearly against the law. George Campbell's gonna see some serious jail time."

"I hope so," Troy said. "He should fry for what he did to Silver. He hurt a wolf that didn't do nothin' but protect itself."

"'Fry' might be a little strong, don't you think?" Olivia asked.

Shrugging, Troy said, "Whatever. The thing I'm saying

is, I hope George Campbell gets what's coming to him. If he gets slammed, that'll be fair. It usually doesn't work out like that. Not in my life, anyway."

Jack didn't know what to answer to that. Was Troy remembering his father and the way he just walked away in his expensive jacket? Or maybe he was picturing his mother. Jack's parents fell silent as if they, too, were searching for the right words. The silence stretched out.

Jack stared outside, at the inky blackness and the trees that whizzed by him like the teeth on a comb. Every once in a while two headlights would appear, beaming into the van before swooshing by.

Ashley yawned. "I'm tired. How much farther?"

"About 15 more minutes," Mike replied.

With a sigh, Ashley curled herself against the side of the door and fell asleep immediately. Her head rolled gently as the van bumped along.

"I can't believe your sister zoned like that," Troy whispered. "One minute she was talking, and the next—" He snapped his fingers. "She's out. I wish I could do that. Every night I stay up, worrying until my mom gets home. That's the only time I can sleep. When she's home."

"Yeah. Me too," Jack lied. Because the truth was, he never worried about such things when he burrowed down beneath his covers. School and basketball practice and thoughts like that might gnaw at him, but that was it. He never once considered that his mother might not come back.

He looked at her, wedged between his father and Mike in the front seat. Olivia's dark hair was haloed by the light of another oncoming car. In his mind Jack saw himself waiting by the front door, pacing like Troy must have done, staring down the clock or willing the phone to ring with a message from his mom. He imagined himself wandering into his mother's bedroom, looking at the clothes in her closet, running his hand along T-shirts and jackets and blouses hanging like empty shells. If his mom died...Jack shuddered, trying to pull his thoughts to a better place. Then he realized that he could do that because his mother was right there, murmuring something soft into his father's ear. But not for Troy. Troy's mother really was gone.

Once again Jack realized the only thing that separated his life from Troy's was pure luck. Luck that he had a dad who patiently taught him how to take pictures, luck with a mother who sang crazy songs from the sixties when she made him breakfast, who could sew up a rabbit's trap-gnawed foot or pull porcupine quills from a dog's nose. Luck with his sister. Yeah, Jack thought, he had luck, lots of it. It wasn't fair, that he had so much and Troy had so little.

"Hey, Troy," he said, "I was just thinking. When we get back to Jackson Hole, maybe...maybe I could help you find your mom."

"Help me?" Troy's eyes narrowed. "How?"

What could he say to that? The words had come

out of his mouth before he'd really made a plan. He'd just wanted to show Troy that he was on his side now, ready to help him the way Troy had helped the wolf.

"I don't know exactly," Jack stammered. He scrambled through ideas that he considered and then discarded. Finally he whispered, "Call a detective, maybe?"

"Detectives cost money."

Jack could fill in the rest of what Troy was thinking. Detectives cost money, and Troy didn't have any.

Softly, so his parents couldn't hear, Jack told him, "Look, I've got $163 saved up for a new camera lens. We could use that. If you thought it was enough."

"It isn't," Troy answered. Then, a beat later, he added, "But thanks. Thanks a lot."

"What are you two whispering about back there?" It was Steven, twisting so he could see them.

"Nothing."

"Well, I want to go over our plans for tomorrow. First thing in the morning, we're going to—"

A high-pitched trill rang in the front seat. The sound startled all of them. Olivia flipped open her portable phone and said "Yes?"

She listened, and said, "Oh, hi, Nicole," then told Mike softly, "It's Nicole from your office. What's that, Nicole? No. No, I haven't received a call in the last half hour."

"What's happening?" Ashley asked, groggy.

"Just a phone call," Jack told her.

For a second, Olivia's eyes flicked onto the rear-view

mirror. She was watching Troy. "What time was that? Uh huh. Did they say any more than that?" Another pause, and then, "Can you give me the number? Hold on a sec. Steven, do you have something to write on? Could you take this down for me?"

As she repeated a string of numbers, Steven scratched them onto a sheet of paper and read them back. Then Olivia closed up the phone. "That was Nicole," she told them. She paused, as if searching for the right words.

Troy stared intently.

"Park headquarters had a message from Jackson Hole. They're trying to contact you, Troy. It's about your mother."

Something inside Jack pushed into his throat and filled it so that he could hardly breathe. He could see Troy's fingers dig into his thighs.

"What about my mom?" His words sounded tight. "Did they find her? Is she—is she OK?"

"I don't know."

"What do you mean you don't know? Who was it that called?" Troy's voice rose higher. "Was it Social Services?"

Ashley was wide awake by now. Olivia shook her head.

"The police?"

"Yes."

Troy blinked hard. "The police called? Okay—then, call them! You got the number! Call them right now!"

"I can't—"

"Then give me that stupid little phone and I'll do it!" Troy was yelling now. Ashley tried to pat his arm, but he wrenched away.

"I'm sorry, Troy, my cell phone just won't reach that far out of the area. We'll have to wait until we get to a regular telephone."

"No! I want to—"

"Troy," Steven broke in, his voice soothing. "Listen to me. We're only a few miles from the hotel. We'll make the call the second we get there. Okay? Just hold on until we know more."

Yeah, Jack echoed in his mind. Come on, Troy. Just hold on.

Even before the van completely stopped at the curb, Troy and Steven bolted out and disappeared into the lobby of the Mammoth Springs Hotel. "I want to go, too," Jack cried, but his mother held him back.

"You stay here," she said. "Give them a chance to find out...whatever they're going to find out."

In silence the four of them—Mike and Olivia, Jack and Ashley—waited in the van, staring through the window at the big front doors of the hotel, wondering what was happening behind those doors.

"Do you think Troy's mom is dead?" Ashley whispered, clinging to her mother's hand.

"Hush," Olivia replied.

The minutes stretched out longer than Jack could

tolerate. "Sorry, I can't deal with this," he cried as he slid open the van's rear door and jumped out. "Troy might need me."

"You're right," Olivia agreed. "We'll all go in."

They saw Steven facing a bank of pay phones. With one finger pressed to his ear, he nodded, then turned and handed the phone to Troy.

Jack couldn't see their faces—just their backs.

Please, Jack said inside his head. Please!

Suddenly, Troy whirled around. A smile wide enough to split his cheeks in half spread across his face as he shouted, "Mom! Mom—are you OK?"

Above Troy's head, Steven nodded at Olivia. "It's all right," he called out. "She's going to be fine."

"Oh, thank God," Olivia breathed.

"The police found her," Steven told them, hurrying over. "I guess she took a drive up the mountains in the rain, and spun out and slid down a ravine into some trees. Her car was so far down that nobody saw her." Shaking his head, he told them, "She was pinned in her car the whole time."

"Was she hurt bad?" Ashley asked.

"Her leg is broken and she was pretty cold, but the doctors said she's doing OK."

"How did she—How—" Jack stumbled for words. "Wasn't she starving? It's been so long."

"Four days. Luckily, she'd gone to the supermarket right before the drive, and she had the groceries on the front seat beside her. She ate hot dogs and drank soda pop for four days. Can you imagine, being pinned and knowing cars were going by and no one could see you and there was no one to help? The only reason the police found her was because she'd blow the car horn about every hour. She knew enough to space the horn blasts so it wouldn't run the battery down. I guess she's a smart lady. And pretty tough."

Troy's voice drifted over to them. "Yeah, I'm with the Landons. I'm fine. Don't worry, Mom, they took good care of me. I even saved a wolf!"

"You know what? This means Troy was right all along," Jack told them. "His mother didn't leave him."

Pulling him close, his own mother said into his hair, "What could be better for any child? He's going home."

CHAPTER ELEVEN

They had to hike the last mile to the pen through autumn-yellowed grasses that rose knee high on Ashley. In the early morning light, leaves from the few aspen trees spiraled as they fell, glowing like golden coins.

"Why are they keeping Silver way out here?" Ashley wondered. "Doesn't he need to be watched over till he gets well?"

"He's better off in the pen," Olivia answered.

Mike had come with them because a representative from the park—preferably someone with the wolf project—always had to accompany visitors to the holding pens. As they walked he told them, "Three of these pens were built in 1994 for the wolves that came to the park in 1995."

Mike went on to explain that after the wolves were captured in the wilds of Canada, they were radio-collared and ear-tagged. Then, after being loaded into shipping crates and flown to Yellowstone, they needed time to recover from the stress.

Ten weeks' isolation inside the pens let them adjust to their new surroundings before release into the park.

"Two more pens were built in '95 for 'the class of '96'—that's what we called the next group of wolves," Mike said. "After that we didn't need any more pens, so now they're empty."

Except for the one where Silver lay wounded. "Careful. Quiet," Olivia warned them as they came close to it. "Don't scare him."

The pen was ten feet high and oval shaped, with no corners, That was because, Mike said, wolves were so strong and so smart they could climb up chain-link fence corners as if they were ladders. A four-foot metal apron on the inside of the pen had kept the original wolves from digging their way out, and had kept other animals from digging their way in to get the meat that was put there for the wolves.

"You go ahead." Mike hung back as the Landons and Troy approached the wolf pen. He was willing to let them savor these last moments by themselves.

"Where is Silver?" Troy whispered.

Steven was busy loading a new roll of film into his camera, getting ready to take pictures when Silver appeared. "Be patient. He's got to be in there some-where," he answered softly.

A large wooden crate stood at the farthest part of

the pen; straw had been mounded in front of and around it for the wolf to lie on.

But Silver wasn't there.

"Are you going inside to check him?" Jack asked his mother.

"No, honey. This isn't a vet's office. And Silver isn't someone's dog. He's a wild animal. The only way I could examine him close up would be to dart him and tranquilize him, and I don't want to do that."

"Then how will he get well?" Ashley wanted to know.

Olivia lightly touched the chain-link fence. Curling her fingertips around the wire, she peered intently toward the wooden crate as she murmured, "He'll have to get well on his own. I gave him a full load of anti–biotics when he was unconscious. I cauterized and stitched his wound. Now we just have to hope for the best. Mostly, it'll be up to Silver."

"But where is he?" Troy insisted. Softly, he called, "Silver! Come on, boy. Let me see you—I gotta go home soon."

Inside the wooden crate, something stirred. Two yellow eyes gleamed in the shadows. Front paws appeared, then a ruff of gray fur, and next, struggling forward on his belly, Silver crept into the open.

"Ooooh," Ashley breathed, as Troy whispered, "Come on! You can do it!"

Slowly the big animal dragged himself all the way

out of the crate. Fifty feet away, on the other side of the fence, the four Landons and Troy waited breathlessly. It was painful for Jack to see the wolf strain forward; bits of straw stuck to his gray coat, which now appeared patchy and limp.

Pushing, fumbling, off balance, Silver tried to stand. With his back paws underneath him, he halfway raised himself on his haunches, but fell over sideways. As he watched the struggle, Jack's throat tightened. And then—the wolf was up on all fours.

A tremor shook his body, but he steadied himself. Raising his head, he stared straight at the humans who'd saved his life.

"He's going to make it," Olivia breathed. "He has heart."

Steven snapped pictures, Olivia wept, and Troy— Troy raised his right arm and whispered, "Yes!" as he gently pumped his fist toward the sky.

"We ought to leave now," Steven said. "Troy's mother is at the hospital waiting for him."

"Someone else is waiting, too," Jack said quietly. "Look over there."

Beyond the trees that lined the edge of the meadow, the black wolf paced, keeping her vigil. Trusting that her mate would return to her, she opened her throat in the most beautiful animal sound Jack had ever heard. It rose and fell, then rose again, seeming to hang on the crisp autumn air until all of them felt they could reach out and touch it—the song of the wolf.

Slowly, Silver raised his head. Softly, he answered her.

As the wolf calls faded, Troy took a deep breath. "We can go home now," he said.

*A full-grown wolf's paw print,
shown actual size*

AFTERWORD

Many would agree that the days now shine more brightly because wolves once again roam the forests and valleys of Yellowstone National Park.

This park is the embodiment of an ethic which recognizes that we are just one part of the land. We have the unique responsibility of having to tend all of it: the forests, lakes, rivers, air, and the wildlife. The Wolf Restoration Program has progressed better than we ever imagined it would. We're well ahead of schedule, we're well under budget, and we're giving the American people something they never expected: a successful program at a bargain-basement price. In this program, more wolf pups have been born, more animals have survived, and fewer livestock have been killed than was predicted. Wolves are thriving in Yellowstone!

Silver, the wounded animal in *Wolf Stalker*, is a perfect example of the animals we're trying to protect in Yellowstone. Once he recovered and was released from his pen, Silver would immediately begin traveling with his mate to establish a territory. There would be an instant rebonding with his mate, and by February, the two wolves would have bred. Silver would be the father of a litter of four to six pups by the first spring following his release. He and his mate would then raise those pups, and the following year, raise yet another litter. These pups would then become Silver's pack.

At this point, some of Silver's first offspring would disperse, and some would stay. Now the pack would consist of Silver and his mate, some yearlings that hadn't left yet, and some puppies.

Silver and his mate would not be the only ones responsible for these pups. There would be lots of baby-sitters in the pack. Most of the helpers would be the pups' brothers and sisters from the previous season, which means every pack member would have a vested interest in seeing these pups do well. As the third year rolled around, some of the original litter, now two years old, would disperse, and the cycle would continue.

A wolf like Silver could expect to live 7 to 15 more years in Yellowstone, and in the park his soul would be well tended. The natural enemies that Silver and his pack would face are few, but powerful. Other wolves and grizzly bears are potential enemies to a wolf, as is every prey Silver would try to attack. An elk is not just going to lie down and be killed; the elk's desire to live is just as strong as the wolf's. It's dangerous making a living in the woods with your teeth! And yet, even with natural enemies, wolves do marvelously well. The Yellowstone area is a great place to be a wolf.

We're trying to restore Yellowstone to what it would have looked like before the area was heavily settled by Europeans, and before Yellowstone was mismanaged in the late 1800s. Left to themselves during these years, numerous wolf packs would have roamed the natural wonders of the park, and their ancestors would be here now.

The young people of today can help ensure the wolves' survival, not by becoming wolf biologists, but by becoming good conservationists who will lead a life that's respectful of the land.

If we want our children and grandchildren to inherit a world that's worth living in, then we all have to make good, conservationist decisions. We can ride our bikes or walk more, recycle, and buy with an eye for the future, recognizing that the things we take for granted are really borrowed from the future. To ensure the survival of a wolf like Silver, we all must live lightly on the land. We must become dedicated stewards who embrace things like wolf restoration.

This book is one step in that direction.

Mike Phillips
Wolf Restoration Program Leader
Yellowstone National Park

Don't miss—

CLIFF-HANGER
MYSTERY #2
Jack's desire to help the headstrong Lucky Deal
brings him face-to-face with a hungry cougar in
Mesa Verde National Park.

Coming Soon—

DEADLY WATERS
MYSTERY #3

RAGE OF FIRE
MYSTERY #4

THE HUNTED
MYSTERY #5

GHOST HORSES
MYSTERY #6

ABOUT THE AUTHORS

An award-winning mystery writer and an award-winning science writer—who are also mother and daughter—are working together on Mysteries in Our National Parks!

Alane (Lanie) Ferguson's first mystery, *Show Me the Evidence,* won the Edgar Award, given by the Mystery Writers of America.

Gloria Skurzynski's *Almost the Real Thing* won the American Institute of Physics Science Writing Award.

Lanie lives in Elizabeth, Colorado. Gloria lives in Salt Lake City, Utah. To work together on a novel, they connect by phone, fax, and e-mail and "often forget which one of us wrote a particular line."

Gloria's e-mail: gloriabooks@qwest.net
Her Web site: http://gloriabooks.com
Lanie's e-mail: aferguson@sprynet.com

The world's largest nonprofit scientific and educational organization, the National Geographic Society was founded in 1888 "for the increase and diffusion of geographic knowledge." Since then it has supported scientific exploration and spread information to its more than eight million members worldwide. The National Geographic Society educates and inspires millions every day through magazines, books, television programs, videos, maps and atlases, research grants, the National Geographic Bee, teacher workshops, and innovative classroom materials. The Society is supported through membership dues, charitable donations, and income from the sale of its educational products. Members receive NATIONAL GEOGRAPHIC magazine—the Society's official journal—discounts on Society products and other benefits. For more information about the National Geographic Society, its educational programs and publications, and ways to support its work, please call 1-800-NGS-LINE (647-5463), or write to the following address:

NATIONAL GEOGRAPHIC SOCIETY
1145 17th Street N.W.
Washington, D.C. 20036-4688
U.S.A.
Visit the Society's Web site: www.nationalgeographic.com